THE
LAST
BUFFOON

DESTROYER
BOOKS

The Last Buffoon

By Len Levinson (writing as Leonard Jordan)
First published by Belmont Tower in 1980

www.DestroyerBooks.com

Artwork by Ayla Elliott
Published by arrangement with the author.

ISBN-13: 978-1-944073-09-1
ISBN-10: 1-944073-09-4

Destroyer Books would like to thank Joe Kenney of the Glorious Trash blog (http://glorioustrash.blogspot.com) for bringing this title to our attention.

For more information on this title, or any of our other titles, please contact the publisher at destroyerbooks@gmail.com.

(Cover photograph posed by professional model)

To Bill and Elizabeth

CHAPTER ONE

RIPELLI PEERED THROUGH THE BUSHES and saw Dominick Passalaqua seated on a lounge chair beside the swimming pool. The old Mafia kingpin had a rubber-tire belly and read the Wall Street Journal, a fat black cigar sticking out the corner of his mouth. Beside him was a pretty blonde doing her nails. In cold hate Ripelli stood, tucked the butt of the submachine gun into his hip, and pulled the trigger. The gun bucked and stuttered in his hand. Blood spurted from Passalaqua's fat gut; he howled at the searing pain. Passalaqua tried to stand, belched great gobs of blood, and then fell to the ground. Ripelli kept his finger pressed against the trigger. Passalaqua's head shattered like a rotten watermelon, his brains flew into the air, his nose exploded down his throat. The girl screamed in terror, the palms of her hands

Riiiiinnnnnggggg.

"Hello?"

"Frapkin?"

"Yes."

"Frank McFarland at Criterion Books. How's the new Triggerman coming?"

"I'm working on it right now."

"When'll you have it done?"

"A few more days."

"I was just talking to the artist, and he says he wants to put a helicopter on the cover. Can you write in a helicopter?"

"Do you want it taking off, landing, or just flying around?"

"Have some gangsters shooting at Ripelli from the helicopter, and have him shoot back. You're setting it in San Francisco, aren't you?"

"Miami."

"I'll tell the artist to put in some palm trees. Speak to you, Frapkin."

"Wait a minute!"

"What's the matter?"

"When am I going to get paid for the last Triggerman? I handed it in almost two months ago."

"I'm the editor, not the accountant."

"I keep calling the accountant, but for some strange reason he's never in."

"You'll get paid, Frapkin — don't worry about it."

"That's what I tell my landlord, but he says he's going to throw me out on the street."

"I've got a call on the other line. I'll be speaking to you."

The connection dies in my ear; the prick has hung up on me again. I return my phone to its cradle, chew my beard, try to pull my concentration together. McFarland and that bunch treat me like shit, but I'll break away from them someday. My great talent cannot be held down forever.

Suddenly a helicopter swooped over the tops of the palm trees. One man sat at the controls; another pointed a machine gun out the window at Ripelli. The hoodlum opened fire, his machine gun explosions echoing across Biscayne Bay. Bullets slammed into the ground around Ripelli's feet. He dropped to one knee, raised his machine gun, clenched his teeth, and squeezed the trigger. The windows of the helicopter shattered and the hoodlum's face disintegrated into a pulpy red mass. Ripelli continued his murderous stream of fire as the helicopter lurched and

Riiiiinnnnnggggg.

"This is Louis Warmflash — how're you doing?"

"I'm broke."

"I thought so. I've got a client who's going to be deported unless she can find an American husband fast. Are you interested?"

"Maybe."

"How soon can you get here?"

"Half an hour."

"I'll be waiting."

I plop the vinyl hood over my typewriter and run through my dingy apartment to the bathroom, where I wash ribbon stains off my fingers, brush my teeth, and comb my graying beard and balding head. Other problem areas are my eyes, which are baggy and hint of misfortune, and my pot belly, a disgusting protuberance on my tall otherwise lean frame. I'm forty-two years old and going downhill so fast it horrifies me.

But now there's a ray of hope — my crooked lawyer

3

might snatch me from the jaws of disaster once again. I dash to my bedroom, which also serves as my office, and open the door to my closet, which serves as my file cabinet. I select my brown Harris Tweed jacket, brown corduroy slacks, and Humphrey Bogart trenchcoat, a genuine Burberry that cost two hundred and forty balloons at Abercrombie and Fitch. From the shelf I pull down my Borsalino fedora and genuine imported French aviator sunglasses from Sex Fifth Avenue. Old Frapkin cuts a dashing figure on the street and soon he'll have money, which is necessary if a man his age wants to carry on affairs with beautiful young women.

I dress quickly, turn down the brim of my Borsalino all around, turn up my flappy collar, and leave my apartment.

It's another cloudy shitty day on Christopher Street, the gay white way where I live. I head east and pass swarms of homosexuals hanging out like vampire bats in doorways, turning meaningful stares into a life style. When I become rich and famous I'm going away from here, because I have a deep-rooted secret fear that this environment, in concert with my thwarted heterosexuality, might turn me into a screaming homosexual maniac.

At Sheridan Square near the subway entrance I buy a *New York Times* and see on the front page that the President of Egypt has made a blatantly anti-Semitic speech in Chicago. An eel crawls up my spine because I have another deep-rooted secret fear that such speeches will bring out the latent anti-Semitism in red-blooded Christian Americans, who'll build crematoriums to settle the hash of New York Jews like me.

Flipping quickly to the financial pages, I look to see how

my one and only stock isn't doing. Back when I had a job I bought, on a hot insider's tip, one hundred shares of the Amalgamated Corporation at twenty dollars a share. I had no idea what the Amalgamated Corporation did and I still don't, but within a few weeks of my purchase the stock began to plummet to three, where it's hovered ever since, but hope springs eternal in my hoary breast and I run my finger down the page that trembles in the autumn breeze. Amal Cp is now at two and five-eighths, down an eighth since Monday, crouching like a lion preparatory to leaping a hundred points.

Folding the newspaper under my arm, I hop down the subway steps and spot a young blonde in a black coat. She glances at me and I flash my best Robert Redford smile, but she looks away quickly. It's all over for me — I might as well sell my cock to a rich old Arab. I continue into the depths of the Sheridan Square station, a ruined man but a great artist, on the way to selling my soul once again.

• • •

My lawyer's office is in an old stone skyscraper on 42nd Street amid the jungle of porno movie palaces and peepshows just east of Times Square. Near the building's entrance is one of the best-stocked porno bookstores in America, and although I promised to hurry, I must go inside to see if they still carry my great porno classic, *Patti's Honeymoon* by Lancelot Wimbledon.

Strolling past the deliciously lewd window display, I open the door and step into the bright interior, full of horny guys slobbering over color photographs of naked girls getting fucked and eaten in various and sundry ways. Like a boy

5

scout following his azimuth, I head straight for the display of books published by Bacchus Press, number one in the field, and see my great porn classic there at shoulder level. Most porno books are ordered once, eventually sold out, and forgotten, but *Patti's Honeymoon* lives on forever, re-ordered again and again for almost three years, and my editor at Bacchus told me it's required reading in a course called Sex and the Novel at a prominent Canadian university. But does Bacchus pay me royalties as stipulated by the contract I signed with them? Of course not. I've discussed this with my lawyer and he said if he succeeded in obtaining the royalties, he'd require most of them for his fee, in which case I'd still be broke on my ass, despite having written the porno novel of the decade. I leave the bookstore and head for his office.

His matronly secretary recognizes me but has forgotten my name. To spare her embarrassment, I remove my Borsalino and say: "I'm Alexander Frapkin and I have an appointment to see Mr. Warmflash."

"Oh yes, Mr. Frapkin — he's waiting for you. You know where his office is."

I walk down a long bright corridor bordered with offices full of lawyers figuring out ways to fuck people over. Warmflash's office is at the end of the corridor because he's a senior partner in this high class swindle operation. I knock on his door.

"Come in."

I open the door and enter. Louis Warmflash, balder than I and shorter, rises behind his desk, a Judas smile on his face, a Tripler suit fitting his beetle body, his right hand outstretched.

The Last Buffoon

"Ah, Frapkin, how good to see you again. Take off your coat and sit down."

I remove my Burberry and drape it on a stand, topping it with my sleek Borsalino, but leaving my shades on. With swift, lithe movements, for I'm quick as a jaguar, I move toward the nearest chair and sit down. Although I appear to be making myself comfortable, I'm ready for anything — as one must be in the office of a sleazy lawyer.

Warmflash has a wet, insinuating mouth. "So you'd like to get married again?"

"If the price is right."

"It's fifteen hundred dollars just like last time, half payable after the wedding, the rest when she gets her green card. And she'll pay for the divorce and all other expenses of course."

"Two thousand."

His smile inverts. "You're being greedy, Frapkin."

"Look who's talking. The price of everything is going up and I've got to live too. It costs fifty cents to ride the subway now, and have you looked at the price of movie tickets lately?"

"But two thousand dollars…"

"Your clients are loaded — they can afford it. Besides, this'll have to be my last phony marriage, and I might as well make it pay. I don't think I could get away with another one."

"That's true — the Immigration people are getting tough. They spot-check homes now, so I'm afraid you'll have to live with her for a few months."

"Live with her!"

"I'm afraid so."

"Forget it — I can't write books with another person around."

"She'll get a job right away, so she won't be home during the day, and maybe she won't even sleep there too often. She's an attractive young girl — she has boyfriends I assume."

"Why doesn't one of them marry her?"

"How should I know? Are you going to do it or not?"

"I'll do it for two thousand dollars, and she's got to pay the rent until we're divorced."

"Frapkin!"

"Cut the bullshit, Warmflash. A resident card is worth that to a rich broad who wants to live in this country."

He sighs stoically, looking down at his hands crossed on his desk. He could've made a great career on the stage, but I guess there's more money in the law. "All right, two thousand dollars."

"And make sure you tell her that I'm a writer and she's got to be quiet whenever she's home."

He raises his hands in the air and looks at the ceiling as if I'm asking him to perform a miracle. "I'll tell her."

"How soon can we get this over with?"

"We'll have to move quickly — her tourist visa expired six months ago. Why don't you meet her tomorrow, go down to City Hall for your marriage license, make an appointment to get married in City Hall chapel, and then go for your blood tests."

"Tell her to drop by my place at ten in the morning. What country is this one from?"

"Argentina." He winks. "She's quite attractive. You might

8

decide to stay married to her."

"How old is she?"

"About twenty-five."

"What's her name?"

"Mabra Valente."

Standing slowly, I give Warmflash a stern look because I know just how low he is — which is even lower than I am. "Make sure she understands that she'd better give me a certified check for one thousand beans immediately after the ceremony, otherwise I'll go directly to the Bureau of Immigration and blow the whistle. And tell her if she gives me any trouble at all she'll find herself back in Argentina so fast she'll think somebody stuck a rocket up her ass."

He stands and holds out his hand. "It's good to be working with you again, Frapkin, despite your paranoia."

"With people like you in the world, Warmflash, paranoia is a sign of mental health."

I shake his hand, do an about-face, and split.

• • •

Four-thirty — too late to go back to the typewriter. Offices are letting out and I'll be able to brush against beautiful young girls on the crowded sidewalks. That prospect cheers me, as does the thought of princely sums soon to come my way, for Criterion Publications owes me fifteen hundred bucks for the last Triggerman, and fifteen hundred for the one I'm writing now, and the Argentine undesirable alien will pay another two thousand. That's five grand altogether, so I think I'll buy some grass on credit. At the corner of 42nd Street and Seventh Avenue there's a cheap restaurant with public telephones inside, along with junkies choking on nutritionless sandwiches. I stroll in and find a vacant phone.

"Yello," says a deep bazonko voice.

"Jake?"

"Yeah."

"This is Frapkin. You holding anything good?"

"Are you holding any money, you fuckin' deadbeat?"

"Not today, but by the end of the week I'll have over a grand. I always pay you. If you can't trust me, who can you trust?"

"Nobody."

"That's not true. I happen to know that you front grass to Harry from Canarsie, for instance."

"Harry from Canarsie has got a steady income, and you don't."

"But I always pay you. Jesus Christ, Jake."

He chuckles, because he likes to break balls. He thinks people are at their best when they're under pressure, which is bullshit, but you have to put up with this sort of thing if you want to buy good herb.

"Okay," he says, "come on over. You got one of your books witcha by any chance?"

"Do you think I'm the New York Public Library Bookmobile?"

"The Public Library wouldn't touch your fucked-up books, but I happen to like them. If you can't pay for what I've got, at least you can bring me one of your books."

"I'll pick one up on the way over."

"When will you be here?"

"Forty-five minutes."

"Ring my buzzer three times before you come up."

The Last Buffoon

I walk up Broadway to 43rd Street and the big Bookmasters store that always carries the latest Alexander Frapkin pseudonymous masterpieces. Entering, I pass browsers crowded around tables where remaindered hardcovers are displayed, then enter a narrow passageway lined with paperbacks. On shelves around me are Tolstoy, Dostoyevsky, Hemingway, Proust, Celine — the great ones. One day I'll take my rightful place among them, but until then I slouch to the crook book section where my execrable masterpieces in this genre can be found.

It distresses me that almost every book I've ever had published, and there are fourteen to date, has had on the cover a man with a gun in his hand, usually taking aim at the poor reader. Exceptions are my porno extravaganzas, which have naked women on the covers, and my Kung Fu fables, one of which is staring me in the face at this very moment: *The Curse of the Green Dragon* by Lin Chung, in which a Kung Fu master is shown splitting a villain's head open with the blade of his hand. I'll get that one for Jake, and here's *Times Square Manhunt* by Emilio Sculangio, number six in my Triggerman series — I'll pick it up too. To tell the truth, I'm rather fond of my Triggerman books. One day my biographers will note their similarity to Greek tragedy, and I'm told they sell well, particularly in bus stations in the Midwest and South, but thus far Criterion has paid no royalties, the cocksuckers.

I carry my two books to the counter, wondering what bookbuyers around me would do if they knew I'm the author of fourteen published novels — a great artist. They'd probably mob me, beg for my autograph, touch my magic coat, and the pretty young girls among them would try to

11

stick their tongues up my ass.

Speaking of pretty young girls, one is holding forth behind the cash register at this very moment. She's a nimble wench with long brown hair and sultry eyes, perhaps I should reveal my true identity to her: Hello there, I happen to be the author of these novels and I wonder if you can tell me how they're selling. If she works in a bookstore she must be a book junkie and might pull down her pants for the great Alexander Frapkin. But I can't say anything — it'd only stamp me as a braggart and a hack. Besides, intellectuals have contempt for books like mine. They don't realize that the great archetypal hallucinations of our times are contained within so-called trashy books, while literary establishment authors like Updike, Barth, Roth — that ilk — are effete dilettantes who should be teaching lit courses in colleges, and in fact many of them are, the scumbags.

"Two ninety-eight," says the brunette behind the counter, casting a disdainful eye at the cover of my Kung Fu classic, perhaps wondering what a cultured gentleman like me is doing with such a piece of shit. Again I'm tempted to reveal myself, but again I refrain from manifesting myself as a fool. I remove my sunglasses, hand her three bills, try to capture her heart with my Rudolf Valentino stare, but she only drops my books into a bag, throws me two pennies change, and looks at the customer behind me, a reeking hippie creep, to whom she gives a big smile.

I'm reminded once more that for Alexander Frapkin, life is an unfair proposition.

CHAPTER TWO

JAKE LIVES IN an old brownstone on Bethune Street, only a few blocks from the mighty, malodorous Hudson River which I smell as I climb his stoop. He's in semi-retirement at the age of fifty — his wife is a top-dollar copywriter on Madison Avenue and maintains the household. He's an ex-pimp, ex-con man, and ex-smuggler who sells drugs of the highest quality to a select group of connoisseurs.

In the hallway of his building I tap his button three times. The door buzzes. I push it open and enter a dark labyrinthine corridor: creaky stairs covered with red carpeting, a polished wood bannister. On the top floor one of the two doors is open a crack. Jake's making sure I'm a friend and not Norbert the Narc, for Jake did five years in Leavenworth for sale and possession of horrible drugs, which is what prompted his semi-retirement and intelligent marriage. When he sees it's only Frapkin the viper he opens the door all the way and holds out his hand.

"How ya doin', man." His voice suggests a barrel of shit being dragged across a gravel pit. He looks like a fat wolf and

13

wears one of those expensive robes his thoughtful wife has purchased for him: velour with broad vertical stripes in yellow, black and red.

His apartment is large, comfortably furnished, and cluttered with the books he and his wife read voraciously. Her taste runs to so-called literature, while he prefers novels of war, crime, and violence. He leads me to a sofa facing two stereo speakers through which a woman is singing:

> *Oh baby*
> *I can't get enough*
> *Of your ooh-la-la*
> *Oooooooo-la-la*

I wish some pretty bitch would grab my ooh-la-la. Draping my outer clothing over a chair, I lower myself onto the sofa. Before me is a round table about three feet in diameter, a nice size for friends to sit around and smoke dope.

Jake sits on the chair opposite me, his stout, varicosed legs visible to the knee beneath his robe of many colors. He always has a skeptical look on his face, as if he doubts the truth of my existence.

"What're you up to these days?"

"I write most of the time."

"Sell your big one yet?"

"Not yet, but I picked up a couple of others for you." Reaching into my Burberry, I withdraw the paper bag from Bookmasters and pass it to him.

He takes the books out of the bag, looks at the covers, and

14

smiles. "Thanks, baby," he says with a chuckle, putting them down on the round table. "What else is new?"

"Nothing."

"You got an old lady yet?"

"No."

He wrinkles his nose, because he has an old pimp's contempt for guys who don't have old ladies. "How come you ain't got an old lady?"

"Because I want a beautiful old lady, and the only ones available to me are pooches."

He points a stubby finger at my eye. "You wanna know why you ain't got a good-lookin' old lady?"

The crap you have to put up with to buy a little fucking grass. "Why?"

"Because you're a recluse, a nut, you look peculiar, you never go anyplace, you're nervous as a bedbug, you're always on some kind of crazy diet, you never have any cash, and you're apt to sit on the floor and start chanting. What broad who's got anything going for her would want you?"

"I'm sure there's one someplace."

"You're a complete basket case when it comes to women, but I guess that's because your momma died when you were a baby. I'm the complete opposite of you — my old man died when I was little and I was raised by my momma. Thanks to what I learned from her, when I was sixteen I was makin' a thousand bucks a week as a pimp."

"I can't help admiring pimps," I confess with a sigh. "They really know how to handle women. By the way, where's the grass?"

"You know what your other main problem is?" He

15

narrows his eyes and cocks his head to the side. "You're too uptight, man. You've got to learn to let the good times roll."

"That's why I'm here, man. Where's the grass?"

Jake gets up and waddles to the kitchen, his feet swollen with gout. Returning with one of his wife's turkey roasting pans, he places it on the table. He removes the lid. Inside the pan is a plastic bag filled with smoking enjoyment. The aroma is luscious and sweet.

"It's top quality Colombian, man. I'll roll a few joints."

He takes out a handful and drops it into a *Penthouse* centerfold of a girl showing the pink petals of her snatch. Shredding the buds between his fingers, he separates the seeds and rolls three joints as slim as nails. He lights one, takes a toke, twitches his big nose, and passes the joint to me.

I stick it 'twixt my lips, inhale lustily, hold my breath, and let the smoke slacken my sinews and tendrils, smooth the texture of my mind. I take another hit and feel myself recovering from the terrible illness known as everyday existence.

"This is some strong shit," I tell him.

"Maybe it's your mind that's weak. How much you want?"

"How much is it?"

"Fifty bucks an ounce."

"I'll take two ounces."

"You got a hundred bucks?"

"I'll have it in a few days. I'm getting married again."

He takes his scale out of the turkey pan. "Another alien?"

"I may not know how to get laid, but I know how to get

16

married."

"Where's this one from?"

"Argentina."

"She good-lookin'?"

"I haven't seen her yet, but my lawyer says she is."

"Maybe if you're cool, she'll give you some pussy."

"Maybe."

He weighs the Colombian, spills it into a baggie, and hands it to me. "You'll bring the bread here in three days?"

"Immediately after the wedding ceremony."

He stands up, the signal that my audience with him is over. I put on my hat and coat, adjust my shades, and put the baggie in my pocket.

He reaches down and hands me the other two joints. "Take these witcha."

"I'll see you in a few days."

"You'd better."

Outside on the sidewalk, night has fallen and I realize I'm starving to death. Shall I have a sumptuous repast in Chinatown in celebration of my upcoming marriage, or should I go home and have some economical yoghurt and wheat germ bread? I decided to compromise and go to the Nathan's on Eighth Street for tasty french fries made from fresh unfrozen potatoes, and then see where my pure Buddha nature takes me. It's only six o'clock, the night is young, and I am beautiful.

I proceed east on Barrow Street, passing tenements and brownstones made of gingerbread and cake icing. In order to see better, I put my sunglasses in my pocket, but also lower the brim of my Borsalino because I don't like strangers to see my eyes. I'm afraid if they do they'll know everything about me, and I want to remain Secret Agent Frapkin. I breathe in deep draughts of the putrid air, and the material world around me throbs and sparkles with the energy of the Tantra. When I'm an old, successful author I'll write sutras to the Lord Buddha, if I last that long.

Through the Village I go, a sinister figure in trenchcoat and fedora, bending slightly into the wind that makes my broad lapels flap. I pass women who look like secretaries, and men with attaché cases returning home from wage slavery in uptown office buildings. I used to dance that jig and know where they're at. They're tired but happy, for they feel their day has been spent in purposeful activity, the poor deluded fools. They're only toiling to make rich men richer, and their miserable wages are never enough to prevent them from falling into debt to other rich men. But there's a revolution brewing — I can feel the sidewalks rumbling beneath my feet right now — and Alexander Frapkin will be in its very forefront fighting for truth and justice.

But first it's time for a few more tokes. I slide into an alley between two tenements, crouch behind an overflowing garbage can, take a joint from my pocket, and light the Flame of Truth and Knowledge. A mangy alley cat looks at me curiously as I inhale a gigantic cloud of iridescent fume, hold it in my lungs, and blow out noisily. The alleyway sags as if made of rubber; the cat sprouts wings and flies away. I don't know who I am, and stroll nonchalantly out of the alley.

A hunger pang shoots across my belly, causing me to realize I'm not an ethereal being. One must eat, wear clothes, have a home, and fuck occasionally. Here's a stand-up pizza joint where the chef really knows his mozzarella.

"A slice, please."

The chef, a crew-cut bruiser, should be a sergeant in the French Foreign Legion. I feel a creation coming on — I'll write a story about a former sergeant in the French Foreign Legion who now operates a pizza stand in New York City. He used to fight Arabs in the Sahara; now he makes pizza on Sheridan Square — how are the mighty fallen. Quick — out with the notebook — I've got to write this down before I forget it.

"Fifty cents."

"Can't you see I'm writing?"

"Write after you give me fifty cents." He raps his calloused knuckles on the counter.

I throw him a buck and continue jotting down the basic idea of the story. This'll be a good one for *Playboy*. Maybe I'll throw in some sex — he's fucking a meter maid or maybe a gorgeous insane model is in love with him. *Playboy* pays three thousand dollars for a story. If they buy it I'll move to California, land of bilk and funny, and write even more brilliantly.

"Make it two slices and a container of milk, while you're at it."

He screws up his face. "Milk wit pizza?"

"If you please."

He thinks I'm a jerk but I need protein because I have a big night ahead of me. I can't let this fantastic high go to waste so I think I'll go to one of those crazy discotheques and swing my motherfucking ass off. But first I need a few more tokes.

19

"Is there a men's room in here?"

"Whataya think this is — Grand Central Station?"

What a nasty disposition he's got. Maybe at the end of the story two black kids in sneakers hold up his pizza stand and knife him to death. He fought innumerable battles against heathen Arabs and survived only to get cut down by underprivileged children. How beautifully poignant. *Playboy* ought to snap it right up, although they've never bought anything from me before, the shitheads.

Here comes my waxed cardboard container of milk and my first slice of pizza dripping with cheese and stewed plum tomatoes. I lunge for it.

"You owe me anudder eighty-five cents."

I throw him anudder bean and raise the slice of pizza to my lips. Rich folks paying thirty dollars for a meal in fancy restaurants uptown aren't dining as well as I am right now. The Italians really have it together where food is concerned — they were busy cooking when Mussolini took over their country.

It's a terrific night. I'll feast leisurely and then get me to the nearest discotheque, where I shall boogie all night long.

CHAPTER THREE

FRAPKIN IN NIGHTTOWN FLOATING through rainbows, passing bars, hamburger joints, bookstores. Frapkin on the move surrounded by young people shining like angels on spit-spattered sidewalks. Automobiles careen like drunken elephants, bums beg for dimes, and Frapkin is the satyr of darkness, disguised in Burberry and Borsalino, his eyes safely hidden behind the genuine imported French sunglasses. Ah, Frapkin, you're the living end.

The Highroller Disco is on Seventh Avenue near Sheridan Square, convenient to all modes of public and private transportation, a magnet for those who want to swing their asses off. At the door is a monstrous black dude in a white turtleneck sweater. I pay him five clams and step into roaring music and drooling lights.

On the wooden T-shaped floor hundreds of drug-crazed young people dance with wild exuberance, propitiating their degenerate gods. I check my Burberry and Borsalino, and, retaining my chromium sunglasses, make my way to the dance floor, where I let the primordial beat transform me into

21

a frenzied Dionysian priest, rocking and rolling in the temple.

I don't know what I'm doing and I probably look ridiculous, but Lord, it feels good. I shake my skinny ass in time to the music, make figure-eights with my hands, and jump up and down, my eyes closed, my head bobbing from side to side. If only we could take off our clothes and have a real orgy.

"Lookit that fuckin' guy!"

I don't give a shit what you think, kid. I don't give a shit what anybody thinks. I'm the Amazing Frapkin and I need this for my soul.

Oooohhhhhh
take me in your arms
and rock me baby

I'll rock you baby, oh boy will I. I do a few authentic Twist steps although that great dance has long since disappeared into the dustbin of history. I do the Stomp, Hully-Gully, and the Madison. Reincarnated as Bojangles Frapkin, I perform my famous cakewalk to the amazement of dancers all around me. For variation I skip through some Lindy steps, a Cha-Cha-Cha, and then execute a spectacular Rudolph Nureyev *grande jete* into one of the rails at the edge of the dance floor, almost breaking my spine. I'd better settle into my basic all-purpose two-step before I kill myself.

I hip and dip casually through three songs, and now I'm getting tired — I ain't no kid anymore. All good things come to an end, but fortunately, so do bad things. Dance your way to the rim of the floor, Frapkin old boy, sit at one of those tables. Wait a minute! Unless my eyes deceive me, sitting at the table right under the blue neon light is an attractive woman about my age, and one seldom sees women my age in these musical fruit bins. Alexander Frapkin will now impersonate Cary Grant in *To Catch a Thief*.

"Hi there. Mind if I sit down?"

She looks up, her hair is long and straight, obviously dyed black. She's been misused and is ready for someone decent like me. "If you want to sit down, sit down," she says. "What do you have to ask me for?"

I sit beside her. "What's your name?"

"None of your business." Her face brightens. "Here comes my boyfriend."

I look up and see a teen-aged black guy in a purple suit and smile big as a billboard. "Let's go baby," he says to her.

She gets up, hooks her arm in his, and without so much as a glance at Cary Frapkin, walks off.

I'm alone at the table, loudspeakers are making my skin pulsate, and I'm plunged into thoughts I've been having for several months now, to wit: The white race is weary, corrupt, and neurotic — we've civilized most of the world, brought about the Industrial Revolution, developed brilliant philosophical systems, invented everything, and now we're running out of steam. The black race is taking over. It's natural for white women to prefer sexy black men over white men who're plagued with doubts, impotency, and self-loathing. It's also natural for rats to desert sinking ships.

I have just had an idea for a fantastic book! Let me get out the notepad and start writing. It'll be a science-fiction novel set in a future where black men and white women rule the universe. White men will be worker-slaves and black women will do all the housework. White girls of exquisite beauty will be gestated in test tubes for the pleasure of black men, and black women will be used as breeding machines for more black masters. But where will more white men come from! I guess I'll make them in test tubes too. This looks like one of my better ideas but I won't know until tomorrow when I go over these notes with a clear head. I'll call the novel *Chiaroscuro* and it's entirely possible that in one stroke the great Frapkin will become the dominant figure in science-friction.

"What would you like to drink, sir?" asks a gay waiter in a red shirt unbuttoned to his navel.

"Can't you see I'm busy?"

"I'm sorry," he says loudly to embarrass me, "but you can't sit at a table unless you order something."

What he hasn't reckoned with is the fact that Alexander Frapkin has no shame. I merely stand up and lean against a wall painted dark red like bull blood. Beneath the blue neon light I finish my science-affliction notes destined to be filed alongside other notes on which I must get to work as soon as possible.

I put the notebook in my shirt pocket as fatigue falls like a light cloak over my shoulders. I'm coming down and it's too early for that. I want to dance some more and come on with beautiful young girls who might have father complexes which I shall help them resolve.

I launch myself from the wall and head toward the men's room where I'll smoke some more dope. I must call Jake tomorrow and tell him how pleased I am with this stuff, not that he'll give a shit. No, I can't call him tomorrow anyway, I'm going for a marriage license and blood tests. Soon I shall

24

step 'neath the nuptial bower once again. Oh God.

Sometimes I think I should kill myself rather than continue these degrading compromises. A handful of sleeping pills and goodbye, Charlie. Many great artists took that route, and so can I.

How can I be morbid with all these beautiful young girls around me shaking their tits and asses? Snap out of it, Frapkin — the force of your talent is irresistible. One day you'll be on top and beautiful young girls will fall at your feet. Greatness flows in your veins and you fucking well know it. These thoughts are unworthy of you.

The men's room smells like a horse stall and is packed with young guys smoking joints, popping pills, sniffing cocaine, and shooting shit. I squeeze into four square inches of vacant floor, pull out my half-smoked joint, and light up. The room begins to spin like the carousel on Coney Island, where I spent my shiftless youth.

"That smells pretty good, man," says a young black cat beside me, his obsidian skin glistening.

"Have one." I pass him a joint. When the blacks take over he might remember and give me an easy job.

He takes it, inhales, goggles his eyes, and passes the butt to his buddy, and thus my Colombian buds begin to travel around the toilet.

"Have one of these," the black cat says, offering me a little white pill.

"What is it?"

"A quaalude."

Eagerly I open my mouth, and the Archbishop of Nigeria places the pill on my tongue.

"Wash it down with this." He hands me a bottle of wine.

I take two gulps. It's sweet and fiery. I smack my lips and return the bottle.

A miracle is happening — someone is handing the tip of my joint back. I take another toke and pass it to the black cat, who tosses the burning roar into his mouth and washes it down with the wine.

"This is really good," he says with a dreamy smile. "Where can I buy some?"

It's seldom that things go so cordially between me and my black brothers. "I'm not a dealer, but here." I take one of the rolled joints from my pocket and hand it to him.

"Thanks a lot, mah man."

It takes me hours to get to the stinking urinals and more hours to drain my vein. It feels like my whole being is squirting out my dick and all that'll be left is a dried-out parchment Frapkin. I'm hallucinating wildly — a black minstrel show is performing on top of the white porcelain urinal, and Al Jolson is on one knee singing:

Ah'd walk a million mahles
fo' one of your smahles
mah maaaaaaammmmmmmmy

I weasel out of the men's room and pirouette to the dance floor, where I see a blonde Juno bouncing her tits and wiggling her ass five feet in front of me. She's wearing a short orange dress and no brassiere. Overhead lights glint on her eyes and teeth, and I can feel her big fat wet cunt rubbing against my face.

26

The Last Buffoon

A robust erection throbs to life in my white jockey shorts, its head itching like a poison ivy rash. I shouldn't have taken that quaalude because they make one excessively horny and now I must have coitus immediately or perish from flaming lust, and I have no wife, no girlfriend, not even a pet cat. Breathing like a long distance runner, I scour my brain for a solution to the problem. I could jump on top of Juno, but that'd lead to a long-term prison sentence. I could engage the services of a whore, but can't afford the fifty-dollar investment right now. So it looks like I'll have to go to a porno movie and jerk off in the back row. Every cell in my body is crying out for cunt, and, oh my God, I'm turning into oil and oozing into this post I'm leaning against.

I must get moving before I pass out. The mad fiend races to the coatroom and picks up his Burberry and Borsalino, then fights his way out of the Highroller Disco to the sidewalk, where young men and women flirt with each other, doing mating dances to the sounds of their hormones. It's so easy for young people — they just go off and fuck. When you get long in the tooth you first must hold discussions to determine whether you agree on a solution to the energy crisis, which liar should be next President of the United States, and various other pressing issues. If you agree on 85% of the issues, then it's okay to fuck.

• • •

I'm on the uptown Seventh Avenue Local. I don't know how I got on board, but here I am. I'm going to get racked up someday walking around zonked like this, but when it happens I'll hold fast to the Dharma and muddle through somehow.

27

The subway car is nearly full and its racial composition is sixty-forty in favor of the dark-skinned peoples. They speak Spanish, French, and peculiar English dialects, and their clothing didn't come from Abercrombie and Fitch. They're loud and ignorant and crazy as us, maybe even crazier, but they're the future and we're the past.

Sitting opposite me is a strange Caucasian character in his sixties. Morsels of his last meal can be seen in his long, scraggly dark-gray beard, and he wears a banker's pinstripe suit in which he's been sleeping and eating for at least a year. The tops of his wingtip shoes are worn through to his greasy black stockings and the knot in his garbage-can necktie looks like a sailor's nightmare, but the most arresting thing about him are his blue eyes, which are intelligent and alert, studying everything on the subway car.

He's obviously one of America's great starving poets. See his sensitive hands, like two doves sleeping in his baggy lap; note his little red nose, with which he sniffs out rhymes. Now he's looking at me unaware that I'm looking at him, for my sly eyes are hidden behind genuine imported French aviator sunglasses from Sex Fifth Avenue.

I can hear his dream songs, miraculous and childlike. His beard is made of flowers. Oh beautiful sir, kindly bard, I'd like to impart a great secret to you, but I lack the courage to approach your magnificence. I'd like to tell you that you needn't starve, wear the same suit for ten years, sleep in fleabag hotels. You should write trash fiction for fun and profit. But you'd never do it — you'd think it beneath you. What you don't know is that the great poetry of our time is being written in trashy books. Take for instance the line,

"He shot him through the room," which I once read in a trashy book written by one of my colleagues. So deep and reverberating. "He shot him through the room."

But you wouldn't do it, oh great master of verse. And you wouldn't teach at a university either, and for that I wouldn't blame you. Writers on university payroll are gutless frauds. They wouldn't know an original idea if one hit them between the eyes.

Oh tender poet, I can see very clearly that you were once Plato, and I, Aristotle, and you taught me sublime philosophy. To show my everlasting gratitude, I'd like to walk to you on my knees and lead you to my publishers, but the train is pulling into my station stop and I must go and jerk off in a porno theatre, for I too have fallen on hard times.

The Cinema Follies is my favorite porno theatre because they charge five dollars admission and thereby attract a higher class of pervert. They're located right on Broadway near 50th Street, nearly on top of the subway station, and tonight they're presenting *Suburban Sex Kittens.*

Tipping my Borsalino low to disguise my features, I slink toward the ticket booth and slip a fin to the dour fat lady inside. She's seen me before. She grunts in distaste and pushes forward my purple ticket to the wonderful world of pussy.

I enter the plush blue lobby and hand my ticket to a uniformed black guy whose demeanor suggests he might be one of Elijah Muhammad's hit men. He tears the ticket in half, perhaps wishing it were on my esophagus, and I enter the dark theatre, where on a panoramic screen, in living color, a redheaded young lady is slurping up a blonde cunt.

29

Len Levinson

It's the Wednesday night early show and there are only about twenty solitary men in the audience, and one couple who'll doubtless go home and fuck like wild animals when they've seen enough. I take my customary seat in the far right corner of the back row, place my Burberry on my lap, reach under it, unzip my fly, take out my handkerchief, cover my cockadoodledoo with it, and wait for the inevitable.

As I watch the tongue job, it occurs to me that I'm seeing one of the greatest all-time cinematic erotic scenes. Usually porno stars do it mechanically, but this redhead is eating pussy like it's filet mignon and she's starving, and her oral skills are dazzling. The blonde is gleefully kicking her legs in the air and squealing uncontrollably, and I'm learning wonderful new techniques which I'd like to try out — right now! Oh how I wish I could be up there partaking of that gazoo, and lo, through the miracle of chemistry I am there, pubic hairs in my teeth and my tongue caressing a blazing clitoris.

I'm whacking my carrot with firm fast motions hidden from public view, and as the blonde comes in my beard, I have a yaaaahhhhhhhhhhh kabooooooooommm out my ears, through my eyes, and into my handkerchief, exploding again and again, my skin drenched with ecstasy and my tongue hanging out. The blonde is quivering and biting her lips, the redhead is licking the blonde's cupcake, and when it's all over they snuggle into each other's arms, and I wring out my cock.

The scene dissolves to the outside of a suburban home, and I have a problem. I've come so much I've soaked through my handkerchief and wet my expensive Burberry trenchcoat. At that moment, the human mind being an odd

30

unpredictable instrument, I am reminded of an old forgotten limerick:

> There was once a magician named Rawls
> who played the finest of halls
> his favorite trick
> was to stand on his prick
> and then glide cross the stage on his balls.

I throw my handkerchief on the floor, zip up my fly, and hand my Burberry over a seat to dry. My genitals feel immersed in the Everglades swamp. Life ain't easy for dirty old men.

The movie continues. A group of housewives are sitting around a kitchen table, drinking coffee and talking about extramarital sex. The dialogue is stupid and the acting horrendous, but the production values are comparable to Hollywood, and the broads are knockouts. Then the housewives go home, and soon thereafter one of them is fucking the paperboy. My cock roars to life and wants some, so I cover my lap with my still-wet Burberry, remove my necktie, wrap it around my member, and soon I myself am fucking that horny housewife in the mouth while she rocks up and down atop the supine paperboy. She gives great head let me tell you — her mouth feels tight and smooth as my fist, and for variation I ram it down her throat for some of that sexy lung. Bazang hisseroony yaaaahhhhhhhhhhh!

In the midst of my copious ejaculation I have the most brilliant idea of my career. It's so overwhelming that erotic considerations are pushed out of my mind by visions of great wealth.

31

I zip up, stuff my soaking necktie in my back pocket, grab my coat, hat, and sunglasses, and run out the theatre to the street, where I stop a taxicab and ell the driver to take me at top speed to that big porno book emporium on 42nd street.

• • •

A half-hour later I'm standing in the lobby of a stone castle on Riverside Drive, pressing the button of Geoffrey Ames, a British guy who directs and edits television commercials and industrial films. I'm about to offer him fame and fortune on a silver platter.

"Who is it?" he asks through the intercom.

"Alexander Frapkin, and I have to speak to you."

"I'm busy right now."

"I'll be right up." I follow an old couple into the lobby and onto the elevator. They get off at the fifth floor and I the eighth. Finding the stairs, I climb the final two floors slowly with Colombian bud joint in hand. When I reach the tenth floor where Geoffrey lives I'm completely out of my mind, which is the only way to be when approaching an important business deal.

I hit the button beside his door and he opens up, a tall swarthy fellow with curly hair, strange Oriental eyes, and a black beard like Satan's. He obviously descended from the great race of Druids who once ruled England, and now he's annoyed at being disturbed by me.

I grab his hand and pump energetically. "So good to see you again, Geoffrey."

He mutters something and leads me into a large living room in which are seated a young man in thick glasses and a wispy blond mustache, and two beautiful girls, one

32

resembling the young Ava Gardner, the other, Goldie Hawn. On the coffee table is a jug of wine and a wooden bowl half-full of grass. I'll bet they were about to have an orgy, the degenerate pigs. The stereo system is making funky rock and roll, and in the dimness beyond his expensive modern furniture are film editing tables, for Geoffrey's apartment is also his workshop, not to mention his riding academy.

"Let me introduce you to my guests," he says, his tone indicating he really doesn't want to. "This is Jim my partner, that's Ann, and that's Stephanie."

I smile, shake hands, exchange bogus pleasantries, reflecting that filmmakers and rock musicians are the artists who attract the pretty girls in this era. I was born seventy-five years too late, but I can't let that stop me.

"Would you like us to be alone?" Geoffrey asks.

"I'm here on business and I don't care where we talk."

"What kind of business?"

"The movie business — what else?"

"Then you won't mind if Jim sits in."

"On the contrary."

"How about the girls?"

"That's up to them."

Ava throws her hands in the air as if she doesn't care if the Russians are on Canal Street. Goldie says, "I love to listen to business," which strikes me as a warped attitude.

"Sit down, Alex," Geoffrey says, resigned to having me on his hands. "Let me take your coat and hat."

"That won't be necessary. I'll only be a few minutes." I begin pacing back and forth on the yellow rug, my Borsalino at its customary angle, sunglasses hiding my eyes, opened

Burberry flapping behind me, and large sperm stain no doubt inspiring conjecture. "I just had a terrific idea while watching a porno film on Times Square and — "

"Which one?" interrupts the sensual Geoffrey, leaning against the fireplace.

"*Suburban Sex Kittens.*"

"Was it any good?"

I point my forefinger at the ceiling. "That's what I'm here to talk to you about." From the corners of my eyes I espy the two girls looking at me as if I'm a geek. "The flick was very good from a production point of view" — I'm pacing faster now — "and its photography was splendid, but the problem, as with all porno films, was that the script was insipid. As I sat there watching" — I crouch to imitate sitting — "it suddenly occurred to me that if a porno film was ever made with a good script, it would immediately become a great landmark film, a fucking classic if you will, and earn perhaps ten million dollars in the United States alone!"

"Porno films don't make that much," says Jim knowingly, his pasty neck being stroked by Ava.

"That's because, as I just explained, porno films are usually stupid. Now listen carefully. Both of you guys have a little film production company and therefore the capability to make a porno film, and I have here" — with a flourish I reach into my Burberry pocket and whip out *Patti's Honeymoon* — "one of the most popular and successful porno books of recent times, written by Lancelot Wimbledon, who in real life is none other than me."

Ava smiles. "Let me see it."

I toss it to her. "Now this is a hard-core porno book with

34

a great story" — my voice is stronger now as I hit the home stretch of my spiel — "and could provide the basis for an incredible pornographic film, the very first to have the participation of a real writer, the very first to be made from one of the most popular and successful dirty books of recent times." I'm gesticulating frenetically. "Let me point out that this very book is presently required reading in a lit course at a prominent Canadian university. I pause to let that impress them, but it doesn't. "Now listen — we can all be millionaires in a year. All you have to do is make a movie out of this book, for which I'll sell you screen rights for a percentage of the profits. You don't have to give me anything up front, and then, with this huge financial success behind you, you'll be free to make the serious artsy movie you've always wanted to make, and I can move to California and continue writing without ever suffering again the nagging horror of my imminent financial disaster." I'm finished, and drop onto a stuffed chair.

Geoffrey looks at Jim. "What do you think?"

Jim shrugs, looks at me, and points to the book Ava is reading avidly. "Can you get us some more of these?"

"How many do you need?"

"About ten."

"I'll call my publisher tomorrow and have him send them to you. Shall I have my lawyer call you about the contract, or will yours call mine?"

Jim smiles wryly, showing crooked horsey teeth. "Let's see if we can raise some money first."

I lean forward and slap my palm on the arm of the chair. "In a few months I'll be able to invest about five thousand dollars of my own money."

"You don't understand the main point of this business, which is to get somebody else to put up the money."

"I know that, but I want to own as much of this movie as I can because it's going to be the porn *Gone with the Wind*!"

"What's the book about?" Geoffrey asks.

I adjust my ass on the chair, cross my legs, and try to behave with professional decorum. "It's about a girl's honeymoon at one of those wild honeymoon resorts in the Pocono Mountains. She loses her virginity to her husband, learns how to blow him, and then proceeds to fuck the hotel manager, the hotel manager's wife, the Chinese cook, the Russian waiter, and various other combinations of people, building to a huge jubilant orgy at the end. I think you'll find it rather witty."

"I'll read it and we'll see."

The room becomes silent except for background music, and I realize that the high point of the discussion has been passed. The time has come for me to make my graceful exit. I stand, adjust my Borsalino, and bow to the ladies. They think I'm a disgusting human being. Beautiful young women are superficial and have no taste, but I'm crazy about them anyway.

I leave Geoffrey's building and head for the subway, exhaustion deep in my bones. My eyes are drooping, a headache is coming on, and I must get to sleep, for on the morrow I must be alert and cautious when the next and last Mrs. Frapkin arrives.

The Last Buffoon

CHAPTER FOUR

I AWAKE ON MY SECOND-HAND WATERBED at quarter to ten in the morning, my mouth foul as a pig's ass. I stagger to the window and peer through the venetian blinds for the weather report, which is disheartening. It's another dark, rainy, windy day of the type that causes me to entertain serious thoughts of self-destruction.

About twenty feet away directly across the alley is the apartment of a Japanese girl whom I often watch from behind my bookcase, and I can see her now; she's elfin and attired in a blue and gold robe, walking around in her kitchen. In the evenings she frequently entertains assorted men and I think she's a real geisha girl who's set up shop in New York City. I'd like to go over there someday and borrow a cup of sugar from between her legs.

The next and last Mrs. Frapkin is arriving in thirteen minutes and I'd better get percolating. I clomp to the bathroom, which is coffin-sized and equipped only with a toilet bowl and shower curtains inside a small bathtub, and take a painful scorching piss. Urinary complaints aren't uncommon for single men my age, but my overall health is still pretty good and in a few days, after this marriage is out of the way, I'll lock myself in my office and finish my new Triggerman. Then I'll start my exposé novel of the public relations industry, or the science-fiction book, or the story about the pizza man who gets stabbed, or maybe something about a Japanese geisha girl in New York, or another idea from my voluminous file of notes.

I shower in lukewarm water because the boiler in the basement is always on the fritz — the landlord likes to make us uncomfortable so we'll move and thereby permit him to double the rent. Landlords are the lowest form of life on this planet, along with automobile salesmen, politicians, lawyers, and editors. In my last Triggerman the villain was a landlord and he wound up getting his head crushed in a trash compacter. At this point I decide to sing that great old Bob Dylan classic:

Hey there, landlord, don't put a price on my soul

The doorbell goes off — gad, it's the new Mrs. Frapkin I'll bet and here I am with soapy balls in the shower. I yank my white terrycloth robe off the hook, put it on quickly, shuffle wet-footed to the door, and look out the peephole.

Standing in the murky hallway is a young witch with black hair down to her bosom, eyes like emeralds, and thin curvaceous lips that I'd like to kiss. I open the door, smile, and say, "Good morning."

"My name is Mabra Valente," she says formally. "Mr. Warmflash told you about me, I believe."

"Yes — please come in." I hold the door and beckon for her to enter my humble shithole.

38

The Last Buffoon

She's about five-foot-two with a figure made for sexual gratification. "Why are you not ready?" She consults her watch. "It is *exactly* ten o'clock." Her accent is Spanish mixed with Nazi stormtrooper.

"I had an important business meeting last night, and I'm afraid I overslept."

Her face is granite. "I expect people who deal with me to be punctual."

"I feel the same way, but sometimes there are unavoidable delays. Please forgive me. I'll be ready in just a few minutes. Take off your coat, sit down, play the stereo, take anything you like from the refrigerator."

"Thank you very much." She unbuttons her suede topcoat and sits on my creaking sofa. She's a good-looking number but there are two thousand clams involved here and I'd better not try anything cute.

I return to the shower and wash my hairy body, shave my neck, and brush my fangs. Maybe when she gets her green card she'll be so grateful she'll blow me. Drying myself quickly, I splash lotions and deodorants on my body, becoming aromatic as a passionflower. I comb my beard and remaining hair and notice with dismay there's a new gray hair on my chin.

In my robe, on my way to the bedroom, I pass her sitting on the sofa. She's wearing plum slacks, a green sweater, and a leather belt with huge silver buckle. On one hand she has four rings, on the other, six. A necklace of tiny orange stones is wound three times around her neck, and her ears are punctuated with silver earrings.

"How're you doing?" I ask.

39

She stops combing her hair and looks at her watch. "It is fifteen minutes after ten," she says coldly.

"If you can't wait a few minutes without being a pain in the ass, go find yourself another husband."

Before she can reply I march into the bedroom and close the door behind me. I dress in antelope corduroy slacks, a tan cowboy shirt, my usual Harris Tweed sport jacket, and nut-brown jodhpur shoes of the sort worn by international airline pilots, or so the salesman told me. I put on my shades and carry my Burberry and Borsalino into the living room. "Let's go," I tell the future Mrs. Frapkin.

She looks at her watch.

"Want to know something?" I ask.

"What?"

"Shove that watch up your ass."

She stands stiff as a soldier, balling her fists at her sides. "I am not accustomed to being spoken to that way!"

"I'm not accustomed to living by clocks. Cut that out while I'm around."

"All normal people try to do things on time."

"I'm not normal. Do you want to go and get a marriage license, or would you rather find a husband who looks at his watch all the time?"

Her eyes become pellets of hate. "I'm ready."

We descend the steps of my tenement, and on the second floor the old Italian ladies in black dresses give us a good going-over, because they usually don't see me with women.

"Good morning," I tell them, tipping my Borsalino.

They mumble and narrow their eyes for they know I'm not Italian. They'd treat me differently if they knew I was

40

creator of the successful Triggerman series, but I'm not going to tell them because they might treat me worse.

On the ground floor of my building is The Corral, a notorious homosexual bar, and already at this time of the morning gay men are there, giggling and goosing each other. Two of them are actually dry-fucking on the fender of a blue Mercedes-Benz sedan parked at the cub, a sedan toward which Mabra is walking.

"Is this your car?" I ask as she takes keys out of her leather shoulder bag.

"It's my boyfriend's."

"He must be doing okay." Then I notice the doctor's parking permit on the visor, from the New York University Hospital. He's doing okay.

She inserts the key in the door and the two lovers glance up. "Oh I'm sorry," one of them says, as if he's just been caught fucking on the fender of somebody's car in broad daylight.

The other one is hostile. "We were just getting into something," he growls.

I shrug like Triggerman. "Well we're driving away whether you're getting into something or not."

Mabra gets in behind the wheel, bends to the side, and opens the passenger door. I slide onto the supple white leather as she starts the engine. She looks very cosmopolitan, very Sex Fifth Avenue. The faggots leap off the car and screech as if it's the Titanic going down. She maneuvers away from the curb and into the traffic.

"Where should I go?"

"Do you know where City Hall is?"

"If I knew I would not ask you."

"Take your first right."

She makes the turn onto Hudson Street, and at my instruction turns again onto Tenth. We drive through the center of the village; a light rain has begun to fall. People scurry over wet sidewalks, around banana peels and wine bottles, holding umbrellas and newspapers over their heads. Dark wet days make me melancholy and turn my blood into sludge. If I don't get to California soon I'm afraid this climate will kill me.

"Are we getting close to City Hall?"

"Not yet."

"Do I keep going straight?"

"You'll turn right on Broadway?"

"How far is that?"

"About eight more blocks."

A cabdriver thunderbolts by on the right and cuts her off, forcing her to stop behind a parked truck. Furious, she rolls down her window. "Watch where you are going — you stupid!"

The cabdriver gives her the finger and keeps on hauling ass. Oh how I love those rotten bastards. Mabra gets going again, grumbling about New York City traffic. She's sexy as a gypsy. I wonder how old she was when she first got fucked and what was the nature of the seduction. Perhaps a blanket on the pampas, some Argentine wine, and a little sticky-finger first. Did she blow him or learn that from someone else? Maybe she's never blown anybody. There are girls who think it's dirty. I wonder if she's ever been eaten properly. If not, I'd be happy to accommodate her.

The Last Buffoon

She steers the Mercedes right onto lower Broadway, a grungy district where Puerto Rican women slave in sweatshops and trucks rumble into congested traffic.

"Mr. Warmflash said you are a writer," she gambits.

"That's one time he told the truth."

"What do you write?"

"Fiction."

"What kind of fiction?"

"All kinds."

"You have had books published?"

"Yes."

"But you are not very successful?"

"I get along."

"You are Jewish, no?"

"Yes."

"You do not have Jewish brains, I do not think. A man your age should be someplace by now."

"I'm someplace."

"If you were someplace you would have a nice apartment and a good job."

"I'd rather write books."

"You must be very immature."

"I guess you think it's mature to look down people's throats and up their assholes all day, like your boyfriend."

She stiffens behind the wheel. "You have not been around nice people very much — I can see that."

"How come he doesn't marry you?"

"That's none of your business! You have very bad manners."

"I'm sorry — I guess I don't know how to act with people

43

from Argentina."

"I am Jewish too, you know."

"I didn't know."

She raises her chin. "My parents emigrated to Argentina from Rumania. My grandfather was a rabbi."

"Were you born in Argentina or Rumania?"

"Argentina."

I scrutinize her features again, and she looks typically Spanish to me. There must have been a gaucho in the woodpile. "Why do you want to live in America?"

"Do you read the papers?"

"Yes."

"You know what is going on in Argentina?"

"You mean the political stuff?"

She nods her head. "Exactly."

"You mean you're some kind of revolutionary?"

"Are you crazy?"

"I was only asking."

"I am not a revolutionary. The problem with my country is that there are too many revolutionaries, and the government is very — how you say — unstable. Also, the Catholics set fire to the synagogue all the time. Also, my mother wanted me to marry somebody who I did not love."

"Make your next left."

She turns left onto Chambers Street, and black clouds speed across the heavens. She has nice legs spread out for operating the foot controls of her boyfriend's Mercedes.

"Do you see that big building up ahead in the middle of the street?" I ask.

"Of course I see it. How could I not see it?"

44

The Last Buffoon

"That's City Hall. Park anywhere you can."

She pulls into the first parking garage. Money is no object to her; I should have asked for three grand.

"Listen," I tell her as we walk toward City Hall, "I've been through this before and I think I'd better tell you that whenever we're around government officials we should act like we're in love, so nobody will get suspicious. That means I'll have my arm around you and you'll have your arm around me. You must try to act affectionately towards me at all times."

She shakes her head and looks at the ground as we walk along. "I am afraid I cannot be that way with someone I do not love."

"You'll have to act a little."

"I cannot do what I do not feel."

"They'll get suspicious."

"Old men like you worry too much."

We walk through the colonnade in front of City Hall and push the revolving doors that lead to the lobby. Inside, we undo our coats and remove my Borsalino. She has nice tits, about thirty-six C's, I'd wager.

"Where do we go?"

"On the elevator." I put my arm around her shoulder.

"What do you think you're doing?"

"Pretending that I'm going to marry you."

"Take your hands off me this second!"

I get in front of her and bring my nose to within a few inches of hers. "Listen, lady — you're paying me to marry you so you can become a resident of this country, and that happens to be against the law. If the authorities ever get wise

45

they'll deport you and prosecute me for fraud and perjury, and I might wind up in a federal penitentiary someplace. Now either you start acting like my bride-to-be or I'll walk out of here right now and Warmflash can find you another stooge."

Her face reddens and seethes with hate. "You have an awful personality," she hisses. "You ought to see a psychiatrist."

"Fuck you, lady."

She stamps her foot. "I am not accustomed to being spoken to that way!"

"Do you want to go through with this or don't you."

She looks at the floor and stutters in Spanish. Then she looks at me. "I have to go through with it."

I put my arm around her shoulder again. "Then let's go."

Her shoulder is soft and warm, her fragrance like tropical flowers. And I have an excuse to cop cheap feels. I wish she were really mine even though she's a little bitch. You have to make compromises when you meet someone who turns you on.

We enter an elevator, ride up a few floors, get off, and walk down a green corridor to the marriage license room, full of loving couples about to enter the holy estate of matrimony. The room is dilapidated and smells like a rotting sponge, but the lovers don't care because they have eyes only for each other. Half of them will wind up in divorce courts like Muriel and me. Muriel was my first wife. We were mad about each other and thought our love would endure even beyond the grave. Two years later she was fucking her old boyfriends and I was considering hiring a punk to put a

46

bullet between her eyes.

I know my way around this room. Taking a form from a pile, I lead Number Three to a table and start filing in the blanks. I learn that her father owns a plant that manufactures heavy machinery, her mother is a housewife who manages a platoon of maids and cooks, and that Mabra lived in Paris for two years.

I hand in the form at the desk, pay four dollars, and am directed to an adjacent room where marriage licenses are typed by civil servants who work at the rate of six words an hour and give dirty looks to whoever crosses their path.

Mabra and I sit on chairs amid twenty other couples, and I put my arm around her shoulders again. "You're very pretty," I whisper in her ear. "I almost wish I were marrying you for real."

She laughs. "That's funny."

I lean back in the uncomfortable wooden chair and reflect upon my catastrophic romantic career. There was Alison when I was in college. She was beautiful, intelligent, a sex maniac, and she loved me, but I got tired of her. Now she's fucking someone else and I'm pulling my pud. Thelma had money and wouldn't have minded supporting my literary endeavors, but I had to screw her sister. Remember Vivian who liked to read *Fanny Hill* while I balled her? I made her so miserable she moved back to Philadelphia.

I never realized I'd be bald, old, and alone.

After a half-hour of depressing reminiscence, Mabra and I are called to the counter and given our marriage license. "You gotta wait forty-eight hours before you get married," says the black lady.

"What for?" asks Mabra.

"In case you change your mind."

"We are not changing our minds."

"You never can tell, honey."

Mabra and I walk arm in arm down the corridor to the chapel office, where we make an appointment to be married in two days. The office is also the waiting room for the couples about to tie the knot in the chapel next door. They're sitting nervously on benches and already have lost the enthusiasm displayed in the marriage license room. On the wall is a big sign that says brides must wear dresses and grooms must wear neckties if they want to get married in the chapel. After Ichabod Crane writes down our information in his ledger, Mabra and I head for the elevator.

I'm having the eerie feeling that I've been through this before with her. Perhaps we were married in a previous life in the temple in old Jerusalem, or a humble prayer house in a tiny *schtetle*, or perhaps I was once Caesar and she, Calpurnia. I close my eyes and try to focus more sharply on the images.

"Are you going to faint?"

"No."

"Then why are your eyes closed?"

I open them. "Never mind."

"I hope you don't go crazy before we get married."

"Don't worry about it. By the way, I don't know if Warmflash told you or not, but you're supposed to pay all the bills that have to do with marriage. You owe me four dollars for the marriage license."

She looks at me scornfully, opens her pocketbook, and

gives me a five dollar bill. "Keep the change."

"We'll need two witnesses for the ceremony. Do you have them?"

"Yes."

"Then all we have to do is get the blood tests."

"I had mine this morning, and I have an appointment for you with my doctor. I will drive you there, and then I have some shopping to do, if you don't mind."

"Your boyfriend will take my blood?"

"My boyfriend is on duty at New York University Hospital. You will see my gynecologist."

Here I am seated in her gynecologist's waiting room, surrounded by ladies from twenty to eighty suffering cunt ailments. In my imagination I see leaky cunts, swollen cunts, misshapen cunts, overdeveloped cunts, underdeveloped cunts, worn out cunts, inside-out cunts and upside-down cunts. It's embarrassing for me to be here, and embarrassing for the ladies because they know I know they suffer from female complaints. The doctor's two crabby nurses have been treating me like I just crawled in from the sewer.

"The doctor will see you now," says one of them.

I enter the doctor's examination room and he shakes my hand buddy-buddy fashion as if he's pleased to have one of his own in there. He has red curly hair and tortoise-shell glasses, a typical overweight uptight Jewish doctor who's playing God, thinks he's a genius, and is doing everything possible to earn a hundred thousand dollars a year. "Sit over here," he says, pointing to a strange contraption where women sit so that their malfunctioning cunts can be examined. I sit and put my feet in the stirrups. Wait'll I tell

49

the boys at Lucky's about this. On second thought, maybe I'd better not.

"So you're marrying Mabra, eh?" the doctor asks, fucking around with a needle.

"Yes."

"Wonderful girl." He jabs me in the forearm, and my precious ruby-red blood spills into his syringe.

"What makes you think so?"

The doctor blinks. "Well…she's a good-looking girl, and she's very bright."

"I'm surprised you let her slip through your fingers."

He laughs falsely. "I'm married already, and I have two daughters. What do you do for a living, Mr. Frapkin?"

"I wrote novels."

"Anything I might have read?"

"Not unless you read dirty books."

"Ha ha ha," says the doctor.

"Ha ha ha," I reply, on the verge of saying something nasty, but my life's blood is being sucked away and I pass out cold in the chair.

CHAPTER FIVE

RIPELLI WAS HALFWAY through the alley when he saw ten of them coming from the other end, moonlight glinting in their eyes and on the baseball bats they carried. He turned but another bunch also armed with baseball bats was behind him. Placing his back against a filthy brick wall, he waited for them, his heart beating wildly, his mouth dry with the taste of Death. They grinned as they crowded around and raised their bats in the air.

The nearest hoodlum stepped forward and swung his bat down at Ripelli's head, but Ripelli dodged, caught the bat in his strong hands, and twisted it loose. In movements so fast they were a blur, Ripelli gripped the handle tightly and slugged sideways at the hoodlum's face. There was a sickening thud, the hoodlum's eyes bulged hideously, and blood squirted out his ears, nose and mouth.

Riiinnngggg.

"Hiya, Alex. This is Roger. Are you working?"

"I can take a break for a few minutes. What's going on?"

"I have a Buddhist monk from Ceylon staying with me

this week, and I thought you might be interested in attending the lectures he'll be giving."

"What time."

"Seven o'clock tonight and every night until Sunday."

"Any broads be there?"

"I imagine there will be, but I wouldn't want you to come just for that."

"Of course not. Is he any good?"

"Yes, and his English is near-perfect."

"Marvelous. That last guy you had — the Chinaman — I didn't know what he was talking about most of the time."

"But the atmosphere, Alex — surely you felt his great spirituality."

"That's why I wished I knew what he was saying. How'd you meet this Ceylon guy?"

"I wrote to the Buddhist Vijara in Washington, and they sent him up."

"This is quite a coup for you — having him in your apartment for a week. You're liable to attain Buddhahood by Thursday."

There's silence on the other end, and I realize I shouldn't have said that. Roger takes his Buddhism seriously.

"You always try to make a joke of everything," he says nasally. "You should direct your energies to higher considerations."

"If life isn't a joke, then what is it?"

"It is pure unbounded awareness. Are you meditating regularly?"

"I've been very busy."

"They say if you're too busy to meditate, you're too busy."

The Last Buffoon

"If I don't stay busy I'm liable to wind up on the pure unbounded Bowery."

"You've got to get over your materialism, if you want to make any real spiritual progress."

"That's like telling a man dying of malnutrition that he's got to stop thinking about food. There are certain material things that people need."

"What a delusion that is. I hope you're in a better frame of mind tonight."

"I'll try to be."

"The point is that you're not supposed to try, but just surrender to the pure white light of the Buddha."

"Okay — I won't try."

"I've got a few more calls to make. I'll see you this evening, and please be on time. It's disruptive when you walk in late."

"I'll make every effort not to make every effort to be on time."

"Goodbye, Alex."

"So long, Roger."

Frowning, I hang up the phone. Roger always treats me like a shithouse rat, while presenting himself as the epitome of wisdom and enlightenment, but I'm tolerant of megalomaniacs, being one myself, and besides, his little Buddhist meetings are good for my soul, particularly since they're often attended by beautiful, sensitive young women who sometimes turn to me for clarification of this or that fine point of the Dharma. Of course I always oblige with a trenchant explanation — and what I don't know I make up.

The one thing that really pisses me off about Roger is that

his very first novel, *Moonlight*, has been sold into hardcover for eight thousand dollars, and into paperback for thirty thousand, and it's an unreadable piece of sentimental crap.

I'm getting frustrated and angry, and before I bust a gut I'd better pick up my handy desk Bible and turn to Ecclesiastes, where I read: "The race is not to the swift, nor the battle to the strong, neither yet riches to men of understanding, nor yet favor to men of skill; but time and chance happeneth to them all."

Yes, indeed, riches don't necessarily go to men of understanding, for if they did, I wouldn't be living in squalor suffering humiliations at every turn, while Roger, who can't get across town unless his wife holds his hand, already has made almost forty grand from a pretentious piece of bullshit that doesn't have even one real human being in it. Goddamn sonofabitch.

What the fuck is that! Unless my eyes are deceiving me, that little Japanese broad across the way is walking around her apartment clad only in her white underpants! It's true — it's her — and right now she's bending in front of her TV set, adjusting the dials, her sinuous ass thrust my way. My schlong twitches to life in my drawers. I fondle it lovingly and wish I could sneak up and backstraddle her the good old American way. Now she's moving to the left of her TV set and I notice the rag in her hand. She's dusting her knickknack shelves, affording me the side view of her small pointy breasts, each of which would fit nicely in my salivating mouth. Oh-oh she's walking away. Now she's gone.

Damn, and she's just my type; I love little broads. I think

there's something particularly erotic about a tiny woman getting fucked. I guess it's the lewdness of the positions combined with the cameo-like delicacy of their bodies, and when you stick your cock into them you don't fall in and find a guy looking for his motorcycle. Hold on she's back! She's taking something down from the shelf and, my God, I think she's going to polish it before my very eyes.

Stealthily, so as not to attract her attention, I creep behind my bookcase where she can't see me, whip out Harry, and start jerking off. Whap whap whap. Her body is exquisite and another advantage of little women is they're light and easily maneuverable, so you can twist them into all sorts of disgusting poses. Whap whap whap. Oh boy would I like to get my hands on her shapely ass. Whap whap whap. She's scratching her tit. Oh Lord, if only I could do that for her. Whap whap whap. She's an Oriental princess and I can just see her blowing me. Whap whap whap. Now she's raised her leg, resting her foot on something. Whap whap whap. I'd like to pick her up and let her down slowly, impaling her right on my oh my oh oh oh oh yaaaaaahhhhhh!

Quick, out with the handkerchief to sop up the goo. Sop, sop, sop — what a mess. Sperm expended this way unites with whatever it touches and produces golems, according to the holy Kabbalah. All I need now is a fucking golem hanging around here. Already I'm feeling tired. Jerking off is such a downer when it's over, but, like the man said, at least you don't have to look your best. When I wrote *Patti's Honeymoon* I jerked off seven times a day and was close to death by the time I finished.

I've just remembered that I'm supposed to have ten copies of *Patti's Honeymoon* delivered to Geoffrey Ames, who's going to make the movie that'll bring untold riches into both our lives. How can my supposedly brilliant mind blank out important things like this? Stuff my softening, dripping scepter of love back into my shorts, I zip up and dive on the telephone.

"Bacchus Press."

"Lou Cohen, please?"

Clickity clackity.

"Lou Cohen speaking." The businesslike voice of a man who reads about five pornographic manuscripts, most of them horrendous, every day.

"Alex Frapkin here. I want to buy ten of my books, Lou, and according to my contract I get them at half price, right?"

"That's right."

"You got a pencil handy?"

"Yes."

"Send them to Geoffrey Ames, 298 West 12th Street, and send the bill to me."

"You still in the same place?"

"I'm not a floating crap game."

"When're you going to write another one for us?"

"Never."

"Why not?"

"Because I get paid more for crime books."

"But you have more fun writing dirty books — admit it."

"I don't have more fun writing dirty books."

"You'd rather fight than fuck?"

The Last Buffoon

"I'd rather get paid more. However I might consider doing something for you if you'd pay me the royalties you owe me for *Patti's Honeymoon*."

"What royalties?"

"You're telling me you didn't sell enough to pay royalties?"

"If you haven't received any, that means we didn't."

"That's bullshit and you know it. I bet you owe me ten thousand dollars at least."

"We wouldn't be in business for as long as we have if we cheated our authors out of royalties."

"I suspect that's precisely the reason why you've been in business so long. Let me put it this way — if you want another best-seller like *Patti's Honeymoon*, you've to pay me the royalties you owe me."

He's silent for a few seconds. I got him with that one. "Let me look into it," he says at last.

"You do that."

"I'll give you a call in a few days."

I'm in shock as I hang up the phone, because it sounds like I actually might have conned him into paying me some royalties. If so I'll pack a bag and fly to Tokyo for a week and fuck little Japanese whores. But I'll have to handle it so Bacchus'll pay me the royalties before I write the new porno book, and then of course I won't write it because if I did I'd have to go through this whole number all over again. Why is it that I'm continually dealing with the dregs of the publishing industry? Where is my Maxwell Perkins?

I look out the window; my little Tokyo Rose is gone. Ah,

57

my dear, how I'd love to discuss haiku with you over hot cups of sake, and then you could sit on my face. Enough of this romantic reverie; I must go out and get some fresh air.

• • •

Near Grand Central Station, I kneel down and pretend to adjust the straps of my jodhpur boots, but surreptitiously pick a skinny joint from the top of my socks. Standing, I light it casually with my Zippo, as if it's an ordinary tobacco cigarette that'll give me lung cancer. Advertising executives carrying attaché cases are rushing about, too absorbed in capitalist deception to notice the dangerous drug fiend in their midst. On 43rd Street a flock of stalled yellow cabs blow horns at a traffic jam ahead on Fifth Avenue, but as the drug takes hold they sound like Gabriel's trumpets. And look at all these pretty office girls, so neat and prim. How nice it would be to have the power of invisibility and be able to look up their dresses, or perhaps hang out in ladies' rooms and watch them pee.

Look up there, Frapkin — the sun is shining! See how it glints on store windows and on the chrome of automobiles. How beautiful the city is today, how exciting, how interesting. I'll bet that guy over there is a U.N. diplomat who's just betrayed his country. I'll bet that fashionable lady is on her way to a tryst with a junkie. New York City is the world's greatest novel, if only I could write it.

Abercrombie and Fitch is only a few blocks away — why not stop in and see all the wonderful things I can't buy? As Secret Agent Frapkin once again, I stub out the joint with a dab of spit, tuck it into my sock with the three other whole ones there, and slouch toward the greatest store in New York.

At the northeast corner of Madison Avenue and 43rd Street the lights are against me, but as a native New Yorker, that's a challenge to my courage and ingenuity. While others wait docile as cattle for the lights to change, the fearless Frapkin charges into the midst of onrushing traffic.

I'm travelling on the balls of my feet, my knees are loose, hips ready to swivel into the tiniest opening. A hornblowing yellow cab bears down on me, but like the great Manolete I dance out of the way and let it pass, while standing gracefully and precariously between its gleaming flanks and those of a black Cadillac limousine. When the coast is clear I dive past the grill of a green Mustang right into the path of another yellow cab, whose driver hits horn and brakes simultaneously while screaming, "Stupid Bastard!" But if I were stupid I'd be underneath his front wheel right now. The air is full of bitter exhaust fumes and my heart is racing as I stand nonchalantly between a scarlet Lincoln Continental pimpmobile and the Riverdale Express bus. As soon as the bus is gone I run fleet as Hermes past a blue Buick Skylark and a beautiful metallic gray Chevrolet Camaro, dodge a brown Dodge Coronet, stiffarm a GM in British Racing Green, snarl at a guy on a Honda motorcycle, and my winged foot hits the curb on the other side of the street. Ladies and gentlemen, the Fearless Frapkin has done it again.

Madison Avenue automatons couldn't possibly understand a man with a sense of adventure, so I won't bother explaining my death-defying feat. Adjusting the tilt of my Borsalino so that it slants even more rakishly across my face and sunglasses, I walk two blocks through a sea of ad execs and secretaries, manage to rub against a few cuties. At Abercrombie and Fitch I step into the odor of leather, tweed, gunmetal, and money. Straight ahead on an old-fashioned wood and glass counter is a display of lamps made from converted moose heads, diving helmets, elephants' feet, and model ships. In the corner is luggage, and I'd like to take that steerhide two-suiter on a jet flight to Tokyo, where I'm sure it would impress the little whores.

Up I go on the elevator to the fourth floor, for an inspection of the very latest in fine Burberry clothing. Racks and racks of tweed, cheviot, hopsacking, twill, plaid, and herringbone. Removing my sunglasses, I'm drawn to a topcoat with a classic bal collar and raglan shoulders, in gray with a subdued pattern of red, green, and brown stripes. Could wear it with anything. Only two hundred and ten dollars. I'll have to get one as soon as I get paid for my last Triggerman, if I ever get paid for my last Triggerman. And look at those wool suits on the rack against the wall. Just the thing for your successful author while entertaining lady friends in his penthouse on fashionable Beekman Place. I could even wear one when I make my first appearance on the Johnny Carson Show. Yes, Johnny, I may be earning a million dollars a month in royalties now, but would you believe I used to walk around in Abercrombie and Fitch in New York completely broke and dreaming about things I'd like to buy?

"May I help you, sir?"

"I'm just looking around."

Fifth floor: the gun collection. Your writer of crime fiction

60

must keep abreast of the latest advances in weaponry. "I'd like to look at a Weatherby .458." Lethal beauty. Smooth and perfectly balanced in my hands, it has a flawlessly performing bolt action and is chambered for the incredible .458 round. It is powerful enough to split a charging elephant in half and is fitted with a Bausch and Lomb scope so you can't miss anything up to five hundred yards away. Johnny Ripelli used this very rifle to knock off Tough Tony Terelli in *New Orleans Bustout*, and he might use it to kill somebody in *Miami Massacre*, I don't know yet.

"Will it be cash or charge?"

"Neither."

On the sixth floor I locate the display of fine tents. I really need a good tent and backpack because I want to go on a camping trip in the Adirondacks and try to get my head together.

"May I help you, sir?"

"I'm just browsing."

"People browse in libraries and bookstores," says this bespectacled old fairy in a gray flannel suit. "I believe you're using the word incorrectly."

"I believe you're right, but I get tired of saying that I'm just looking around."

"I quite understand, and I hope you won't think me overly critical."

"On the contrary, I'd like to thank you for pointing out my error. Precise speech encourages precise thinking."

The old fairy smiles graciously, showing a mouthful of false teeth that nearly blinds me. "I go off duty in a half-hour. Do you think we could meet for a drink?"

"I'm afraid not, I have a previous engagement."

"Some other time perhaps?"

"Perhaps."

I tip my hat and head for the elevators.

On the seventh floor, in the boating section, I grip the spokes of a five hundred dollar ship's wheel made of teak, and imagine myself steering a PT boat across the stormy North Atlantic, my hold filled with the very finest Lebanese hashish, a pack of Nazi U-boats trying to track me down, and Raquel Welch, clad in only high-heel shoes and French perfume, in the galley preparing sautéed bean sprouts. I reach toward a large brass ship's bell costing two hundred dollars, grasp the rope, and shake it back and forth, clang clang clang, calling my crew to general quarters, and then realize to my horror that I'm in Abercrombie and Fitch actually clanging a ship's bell, freaking out once again in a public place under the influence of insidious drugs.

I glance around cautiously and see every single person on the floor looking at me with surprise and malevolence. A blue-suited, very correct gentleman with the air of an admiral of the fleet, marches toward me.

"May I help you, sir?"

"The tone is too high-pitched for my boat," I say with absolute drug-crazed assurance.

That stops him cold. Rich eccentrics often shop at Abercrombie and Fitch. "We could order one for you in any tone you like."

"I'd like one two octaves lower and in the key of G."

He's writing on a pad. "Your name, sir?"

"Lancelot Wimbledon."

The Last Buffoon

"Your address?"

"Eight-twenty-one Park Avenue."

I walk casually to the elevator and in my peripheral vision see certain faces I've observed on every floor throughout the store. They must be the plainclothes security force following me around because they suspect I'm a dangerous weirdo, which is certainly true and just demonstrated with the ship's bell. I've got to get out of here before they stop me and find two and one-third joints of fine Colombian buds in my sock, sufficient evidence to lock me in Attica for fifty years.

I polish my sunglasses with my dirty handkerchief until an elevator comes, ride down to the ground floor, and make a beeline for the nearest exit.

That was a close call — fucking jackass bastards are everywhere and they have the power to do horrible things. The world is full of pigs! Now hold on. Wait a minute there, Frapkin. You know very well that you can't blame people for being what they are, because they're impelled by hidden forces too. You've got to love your fellow man and your enemy even when he smites you, for the hand of the Lord is behind everything, and your brain is too puny to comprehend His Divine Design.

That's right — sometimes when I'm frightened I forget. Even Yasser Arafat must be understood and loved, for he's only trying to help his people, even if he has to kill everyone else to do it.

How fortunate I am to be having spiritual thoughts only six blocks from Saint Patrick's Cathedral. I think I'll stop there, kneel before the statue of Jesus Christ, and receive holy inspiration.

63

In order for the experience to be truly profound, I'd better smoke another joint. I stop in the doorway of a hatter, pull out a fresh joint, light it up, and continue on my merry way. This is such good dope, and I have so much of it. Maybe I should throw a party. No, my friends would smoke it all in one night, vomit on my floor, insult me, and then I'd have to buy more. At 50th Street I turn the corner and straight ahead is Saint Patty's, a great gothic fortress of God, right across the street from Sex Fifth Avenue.

Up 50th Street I go, passing Fifth Avenue windows full of gorgeous mannequins in five hundred dollar dresses. Maybe I should buy one of those mannequins, drill out the vaginal area, stuff it with warm wet sponge, and fuck all night long.

I cross the street, and on the wide front steps of the cathedral and snuff out the joint. A young guy in a beard winks at me and I wink back — one dope fiend can always recognize another. Okay, get set, in you go, Frapkin old boy.

I climb the steps, pass quickly through the lobby, and enter the vast cathedral. Sweet frankincense touches my nose, candles flicker everywhere, and straight ahead is the shining altar where the Archbishop of New York celebrates mass. This place always gets to me; my heart swells with the spirit of the Lord. I stand in line at the fountain and when my turn comes, cross myself with holy water and mumble, "In the name of the Father, the Son, and the Holy Ghost, Amen." Next I proceed down the main aisle, passing rows of wooden benches where Catholics are praying. Granite columns soar up around me in arches high above, where angels and cherubs sing choruses of hallelujah. This has to be the most magnificent room in the world, truly the house of

64

the Lord.

Jewish religious fanatics would consider me a traitor for being here, but the pious Frapkin has a heart and mind that can embrace the truth of all the world's great religions. How can I deny one who said, "Blessed are the poor in spirit, for theirs is the kingdom of heaven"? He was talking about folks like me when he spake those words.

I make my way to a tiny dark area behind the altar, where a spotlight shines on a life-sized statue of Jesus Christ nailed to the cross. Blood drips from his thorn-crowned head and his pierced hands and feet. His eyes look to the heavens, and he says, "Forgive them, Father, for they know not what they do." I drop a quarter in the box and light a candle for the beleaguered people of Israel, who produced the great rabbi Jesus Christ, before whom I kneel to pray.

Oh, Great Rabbi Jesus, help me to love those who hate me, for I know only Love can solve the terrible problems of the world. Please help me to be strong in my faith, help me to understand the hideous things I do, help me to persevere, and thank you for suffering my stupid presence these few minutes. Amen.

A little religion goes a long way with me, and I need a drink. The bars around here are full of executive sissies, and a bottle of fine Guinness Stout probably will cost five dollars, or maybe I'd better head west toward Times Square.

But first I think I'll smoke another joint. I leave the cathedral, stop across the street near the entrance to a Rockefeller Center building, pull out a fresh one, light up, and continue on my way. As I near the Rockefeller Plaza skating rink, I hear the strains of Strauss' *Tales From Vienna Woods*.

Look at all the nice skaters gliding gracefully over the ice, the ladies wearing short skirts, the gents as 19th century aristocrats. It looks like fun but if I went down there like this I'd break my ass for sure and I'm in bad enough shape as it is. Dig the legs on the little blonde in the pale blue sweater. She can wrap them around my neck anytime, and farther down Fifth Avenue — hold on — in front of a fancy ladies dress shop there stands a foxy lady, maybe thirty-five years old, wearing a long leather coat, and she looks like a famous Broadway actress. Like Warren Beatty I stroll over, smile suavely, and say, "So I've found you at last."

Her long eyelashes paint the air. "I beg your pardon."

"I said I've found you at last."

"I think you've got me mixed up with somebody else." She looks away.

I sidestep into her line of vision. "Let's have a drink together in that quiet little place around the corner."

She levels a withering stare at me. "Mister, I don't know what your problem is, but if you don't leave me alone I'm going to call a policeman."

I tip my hat, turn, and move away fast. The Nos don't count — only the Yesses do. A great cocksmith from Brooklyn told me that once, it's been my credo ever since. Besides, I really don't know any quiet little place around the corner.

I plunge into the unfashionable West Side via 45th Street. When I was a public relations dude, my office was on the next block. Maybe I should go over and see the old gang. Perhaps I could borrow a tenner from my old boss. No — that isn't one of my better ideas. It'd be humiliating to go begging over there, and when they ask what I'm doing, what can I say? That I've written fourteen trashy novels since I left them? Keep on truckin', Frapkin my man.

After crossing Sixth Avenue, 45th Street becomes two rows of topless bars, massage parlors, and cheap hotels where the troopers of whoredom conduct their social work. Fate seems to have led me here so I think I'll stop in one of these dives for some good Guinness Stout and tits-and-ass before dinner. But which dive? I read signs on both sides of the street: CAROUSEL BAR, PONY LOUNGE, POLKA DOT CLUB, KENNY'S PARADISE, THE DIAMOND NECKLACE, CHEZ FIFI, HOLLYWOOD PUB, THE PALACE OF SCHEHERAZADE.

The Palace of Scheherazade stimulates my novelist's imagination. I visualize an Oriental parlor filled with nymphomaniac dervishes. It's halfway down the block on the other side of the street. I cross over, clip-clop toward it, push open the door, and step inside.

There are colored balloons hanging from black walls and the ceiling, and red spotlights fixed on young girls in G-strings and spiked heels dancing on platforms above the long bar. The music is loud rock and roll.

"Hiya, fella," calls the dancer near the door, a redhead with long eyelashes.

"Hiya, baby." I give her a Jack Nicholson smirk. I stand near the door and case the joint. Business is slow this time of the afternoon so I'll be able to sit next to the platform on which is dancing the prettiest girl in the place, a Latin number with black hair almost down to her waist, about five feet four inches tall, in complete confident possession of a

67

perfectly proportioned body. The classic beauty of her face indicates she was an Aztec princess in a past life, and here she is dancing away the afternoon in a crummy topless bar probably owned by the Mob. I stroll forward and sit on the stool next to her.

A chubby, bleached-blonde barmaid in black tights and mesh stockings walks up to me. "Whataya want?"

"That girl's phone number." I point my thumb at the Aztec princess.

"Don't be a wise guy." She looks down the bar at a gorilla in a shiny green suit, the bouncer.

"A Guinness Stout, please."

She screws up her gun moll face. "A what?"

"A Guinness Stout — it's a kind of beer imported from Ireland."

"The only beer we got here is Rheingold."

"Lemme have one."

She shuffles toward the beer cooler, and damnit, I really want a Guinness. Regular beer is made with hops and is bitter to my sensitive artistic tongue which would like to lick the Aztec princess from toenail to hairline right now.

"Is that Alexander Frapkin?" somebody yells.

Startled, I turn in the direction of the voice and see Mike Brown, one of the sharp young press agent fiends from my old office, walking toward me from the back of the place. Last time I saw him was a few years ago at a party in the Village where somebody got stabbed.

"How ya doing, you old sonofabitch!" he yells, shaking my hand as I stand. He's got black hair, is smooth shaven, wears a dark suit, and looks untrustworthy.

The Last Buffoon

"Not bad. How're you doing?"

"Terrific!" He withdraws his hand and motions to the barmaid. "Bring my friend a drink."

She holds up the bottle. "Whataya think I'm doin'?"

He looks at me. "You're drinking beer?"

"Yes."

He looks at the barmaid. "Bring him a double-shot of Johnny Walker Black on the rocks, and bring my Jack Daniels over here." He throws a tenner on the bar and winks at me. "I'll charge it to one of your old clients. What're you doing in here?"

I sit back down on the stool. "I happened to be walking by and I was thirsty. How about you?"

"I was on my way back to the office, and I thought I'd better have a drink first. I've been snorting coke all day and you know how you get sometimes — my teeth were starting to buzz. My old lady happens to work here too."

"Who's your old lady?"

"The one dancing beside you."

"That's your old lady?"

"Yep."

"She's very pretty, man."

"You bet your ass. You want a little of the cocaine?" He pulls his wallet from his back pocket, extracts a folded bill an inch square, and hands it to me. "The men's room is back there I just came from."

I head in that direction, pass the gorilla I intend to use soon in a Triggerman book, and enter the tiny men's room. Stepping inside the one toilet stall, I close the door behind me, unfold the bill, and look inside at the snow of the

69

Andes. I take out my keys, select one for use as a spoon, dig in, gingerly carry the tiny mound of coke to my right nostril, and snuff it into my brain. My nose and throat go numb instantly and a few seconds later I'm twenty pounds lighter and energetic as Muhammad Ali. I repeat the process for my left nostril, and I'm fifty pounds lighter, strong as four Muhammad Alis.

I swagger back to Mike and hand him the bill. "Thanks, baby."

"How's your head?"

"Beautiful."

The barmaid has served my Johnny Walker. I lift the glass and take a slug, then sit down. Deep in my chest a hydroelectric dam is producing a billion kilowatts every second, and Mike's eyes are glittering like bowls of jewels.

He sips some Jack Daniels straight out of a shot glass.

"How're you doing these days?"

"I'm getting along."

"Publish anything yet?"

"A few trashy books — nothing special."

"Making any money."

"A little."

"You don't look so good — I hate to say it."

"I'm forty-two years old, and time takes its toll."

"Forty-two years old isn't old."

"You'll find out for yourself in a few years what's old and what isn't. At first you'll think maybe you're not eating right or that you've got cancer, so you'll see a doctor and he'll tell you nothing's wrong. Then you'll realize it's old age creeping up."

The Last Buffoon

"Bullshit — I bet I know what you need. You should come back to the office and start wheeling and dealing again. We could work on the same accounts and have a ball."

"That's all over for me."

"You're nuts."

"So I'm nuts."

"How can you do something that's ruining you?"

I rest my glass on the bar and try to marshal my thoughts. "Do you know what it's like when you're running a stunt and it's going great and you've got the *Times*, the *News*, and the *Post* there, and all the TV network cameras, and all the wires, and you know that you'll probably get a raise out of it, and some cute broad from an obscure French news syndicate is sending out signals that she wants to make it with you. Do you know what I'm talking about?"

"Sure I do."

"Well writing books, even my crappy ones, is better than that."

"It really is?"

"That's right."

"Then go to it, baby."

"I am."

He takes a sip of booze, then touches the back of his hand to my gut. "Hey — why don't we drink up and go back to the office. A lot of the old bunch is still there and they'd love to see you."

"I don't feel like going up there."

"C'mon."

"Nah."

"Your secretary Ethel is still there. You can pull her chain."

"Some other time, maybe."

The music stops, the three dancers descend the spiral staircases connecting their platforms to the floor, and the next shift of dancers climbs up. The Aztec princess walks toward Mike, her bare boobs stick out as only books can.

"Hi, baby," she says.

"Hi."

They look intimately at each other but don't kiss because I guess that's against the rules of the house.

"Suzie, this is an old buddy of mine, Alex."

The music starts up again. "Hi, Alex."

"Hello, Suzie."

"Isn't she incredible?" Mike asks.

"She's even better than incredible."

The loudspeakers blast a raucous version of *Night Train*. The replacements punch the air and wiggle their asses. Mike takes out his cocaine bill and hands it to Suzie. She takes it, murmurs goodbye to me, and hipshakes to the dressing room.

"I really dig her," Mike says, "but not so much that I don't know what I'm doing." The red lights make a sheen on his dimpled chin. "She's a talented little girl. I'm going to start managing her career. You were just talking to the next Brigitte Bardot."

"I'll be able to say I stood next to her when."

He smiles and holds out his hand. I slap it.

"Who're you going out with these days?"

"Nobody."

He looks surprised. "Nobody?"

"That's what I said."

72

"How come?"

"I haven't got any bread. To mess with broads you need bread."

"It probably wouldn't hurt if you shaved off that beard. You look like one of the Smith Brothers."

"I thought it made me look a little like Ernest Hemingway."

"I'm afraid not, man."

I take another sip and look mournfully at the rhinestone snatch of a willowy blonde dancing four feet from us.

"I never thought I'd see the day when the guy who called himself the New York Flash wouldn't have a broad going for him," Mike says.

"You've seen the day."

"I remember that German actress you used to go with. What was her name?"

"Frieda."

"Yeah, Frieda. What happened to her?"

"She went back to Germany — who the fuck knows?"

"How about the model? The one with red hair?"

"We broke up a long time ago."

He shrugs. "I wish I knew what to tell you, man."

"There's nothing to say." I look at my watch. "Listen — I've got to get going."

"What's your hurry?"

"I gotta see a guy about something." Lifting my drink, I drain every drop.

"Gimme a call sometime."

"Okay."

"You won't."

73

"Neither will you." I shake his hand. "Take it easy, Mike."

"You too, Frap."

I adjust my Borsalino, turn, and walk past prancing girlflesh to the door.

• • •

A scoop of cottage cheese and a salad at the Automat, then subway uptown. Some young black kids are screaming and jumping, terrorizing all the good white folks around them on the subway car. I hope they don't bother me because if I should belt one I'd be branded a racist pig and hung at down.

My encounter with Mike has disturbed me, because it's reminded me of happier days. It'd be great to have a big pad and be a sharp guy again. I'd buy some French suits and loaf in nightclubs, talk shit and get a little bit. Beautiful women can't resist superficial guys who throw money around. I know my old boss'd love to have me back. I probably could get four hundred a week out of him, and steal another fifty form my expense account. But do I really want to do all that again? I don't think so.

• • •

"You're late again," says a tight-lipped Roger, looking at his watch and running his hand over his shaved head.

"I had a very important business appointment."

"You've been drinking."

"I only had a couple."

He shoots me one of those looks that says, You're polluting my high level of consciousness, then leads me into his candlelit living room, where about twenty people are sitting on cushions around a little brown gnome in a saffron

74

robe. Roger's roly-poly wife smiles at me. The Buddhist gnome bows and says, "Hello."

I bow back. "I'm sorry to be late, sir."

He motions to an empty cushion, and by a cosmic stroke of luck, it happens to be next to a brunette with big tits and a cute face, who's seated in the lotus position. I'd like to demonstrate certain fine points of acupressure for her, but then I notice she's near a bearded guy so emaciated and pale he must be in the terminal stages of an awesome fast. She's probably in love with the jerk. My head swimming with cocaine, beer, scotch, and marijuana, I sit cross-legged on her other side, but am unable to assume the full lotus because I'm not made right.

The monk continues his lecture. "And so we see," he says in his curiously accented, somewhat feminine voice, "that Buddhism is fundamentally a meditation that helps show us the false nature of conceptual thought, which, as I have tried to explain, is the source of all hatred, selfishness, suffering, and delusion."

An academic type in a seedy tweedy jacket, raised his hand.

"Yes?" asks the monk.

"Isn't what you just said a concept itself?"

"It is the denial of concepts."

"I think you're making a false distinction."

"It is a delusion to think *I*, because that is a concept too."

I raise my hand, causing Roger to make a pained expression that says There he goes again — why do I invite him here?

"Yes?"

"I don't understand how it can be a delusion to think of ourselves as *I*," I say. "If we don't think of ourselves as *I*, how can we function in the world?"

"We function in the world by practicing Buddhist meditation."

"But I'm here, I'm sitting in front of you. Isn't that so?"

"It is so that something is there."

"That something is me. I am here."

He shakes his head no.

"Then what is here?" I ask.

He smiles and says softly, "Ignorance."

76

CHAPTER SIX

LORD GOD ALMIGHTY, I'm in the City Hall chapel getting married again. The room is small, bare, and pale green. I can hear the sound of traffic from the street outside.

Behind a lectern is Marryin' Sam: chinless, hairless, and humorless, dressed in a baggy blue suit with unfashionable narrow lapels. He considers his job a very weighty matter, as well he should.

In attendance as best man is Dr. Sidney Siegel, Mabra's boyfriend, who has short curly black hair, the build of a welterweight, and the confidence that comes from a high-paying job. He's photographing the proceedings with his thousand-dollar Leicaflex.

The maid of honor is Cecille, a petite French girl who either has to go to the bathroom or is late for an appointment somewhere else.

"Do you, Mabra, take this man Alexander, to be your lawful wedded husband, to love and to cherish, in sickness and in health, in good times and in bad times, for better or worse, till death you do part?"

77

"I do," she replies with a little smile intended to show her boyfriend and Cecille that it's all a joke.

"I pronounce you man and wife," says Marryin' Sam, and a chill passes through my body. His official features soften for the first time. "You may kiss the bride."

If he says it's okay I guess I can do it. I bend over Mabra's uncertain smile and slide my tongue through her lips and between her teeth. She pulls back but then freezes, realizing women don't try to escape the wedding kiss. Our tongues rest together and the yin and the yang have become one. I don't want to overdo this. Slowly I draw back, a little wobbly in the knees.

Marryin' Sam opens the door to the waiting room and gives the clerk the high sign. The clerk, the same Ichabod Crane who signed us up two days ago, reads names from a list, and four Puerto Ricans get up and move — their great moment has come.

We pass through the waiting room and enter the corridor that leads to the elevators. Dr. Sidney Siegel, his red silk tie coordinating beautifully with a gray flannel suit, snaps his Leicaflex into its case. I'm wearing a glen plaid suit I bought at Paul Stuart's ten years ago.

"I've got to get back to the hospital," Dr. Siegel says. "Can I give anybody a lift someplace?"

"I have classes this afternoon," says Cecille, who's previously identified herself as a student of the English Language at Columbia University.

"I'll drop you at the subway," says generous Sidney.

"I have to buy some things to clean his apartment," Mabra says. "It is a pigpen."

78

"I'll drop you at a supermarket."

"Remember to leave my desk alone," I warn Mabra.

"You will be home this afternoon?"

"I don't know."

"How will I get in if you are not home?"

"With the keys I made for you." I reach into my pants pocket and hold them up. "That's the one for the downstairs door, that's for the mailbox, that's for the fire escape, that's for the top lock on my door, and that's for the police lock. Always keep the door locked because the neighborhood's crawling with burglars and rapists." I hand her the keys, then unsling my hat and coat from my arm and put them on.

Dr. Sidney Siegel scratches his cheek. "May I have a few words with you alone, Alex?"

"Sure, Sid."

The women walk toward the elevator and the doctor and I stand against a closed door.

"Mabra is sort of a high-strung girl," he says. "I hope you don't do anything that might upset her."

"What did you have in mind?"

"Well, she's a pretty girl, and we hope you wouldn't try to take advantage of the situation."

"I'm doing this for the money. Where is it, by the way?"

He reaches into the inner breast pocket of his immaculate suit, pulls out an alligator wallet, removes a check, and hands it to me. It's a Manufacturers Hanover Trust money order made out to me from Charles Jones.

"Who's Charles Jones?"

"A fictitious name. We don't want anybody to trace the money to us."

I slide the check into the inner pocket of my old press agent suit, my spirits suddenly improved.

"Do I have your word that you won't try anything with Mabra?"

"If you're so worried, why didn't you marry her?"

He raised his eyebrows as if I've suggested he transplant a frog's heart into a man's toe. "Mabra and I don't believe in marriage. We feel it would complicate our relationship."

"I see. Well, I'll keep my hands off her if she'll keep her hands off me."

"I don't think we have to worry about that."

He turns to walk away, but I grab his shoulder. "By the way, I was wondering if you could do me a favor."

"What kind of favor?"

"I need a prescription for some quaaludes."

"Do you have a nervous condition?"

"You mean you haven't noticed?"

"It's a lot of trouble to write a prescription for quaaludes. I have to send copies to the state and local police."

He starts to move away but I grab him by the shoulder again. "How about valiums?"

He sighs. "Okay, I'll write you a prescription for valiums."

"Put some Dalmanes in the prescription too, because I have trouble falling asleep sometimes, and some Dexedrine, because some times I have trouble waking up."

He looks at me sternly like a doctor-genius-god. "Are you a pillhead, Alex?"

"I'm a sick man."

"I don't have my prescription pad with me. I'll write it in my office and give it to Mabra."

"Fine."

We walk toward the girls, who're waiting near the elevator. My wife looks irritable and we've only been married ten minutes.

"I'd like to speak with Alex alone please," she says, smiling coldly at Dr. Siegel.

A shadow passes over his face. "Very well."

Mabra walks to my side and we return to the door. I lean against it, she crosses her arms.

"What did he say to you?" she demands.

"If you want to know — ask him."

She speaks through tightened teeth. "I'd be very grateful if you told me what he said."

I don't like to be a stool pigeon, but to hell with Dr. Sidney Siegel. "He asked me not to try and screw you."

She turns the color of boysenberry yoghurt. "I see."

"I can't help but be impressed by the great love and trust that exists between you two."

"Please mind your own business."

My wife turns and walks toward the doctor and Cecille, through wedding parties drifting back and forth in the corridor. I follow and say, "I wonder if I might speak with Cecille alone for a moment?"

The three look at each other. Little Cecille, who has short black hair and a neat figure, steps forward and accompanies me to the door.

"What ees eet?"

"I was wondering what you were doing after classes today."

"Why you care about zat?"

"I thought maybe we might have a drink, or a smoke, or a pill together."

"You and me?"

"Oui."

"You are not joking?"

"Not at all — I've always had a thing for French girls."

"Well, I do not have a thing for you. Goodbye."

She turns and walks to the elevator, and I follow. Dr. Sidney Siegel looks like his favorite patient just died. "Can I drop you somewhere, Alex?"

"No thanks, but please don't forget to give Mabra that prescription." I smile at all of them. "Good day." Pushing open an exit door, I race down a flight of stairs, displaying my flair for drama once again.

"What would you like, cherie?" asked Cecille.

"You got any scotch?"

"But of course."

"A little over ice, if you don't mind."

Cecille gave his dick a tender kiss, rolled out of bed, and walked naked to the kitchen. Ripelli lit a cigarette and blew smoke at the ceiling, hoping the little French bitch could lead him to Don Salvatore Castelango.

She returned, holding a glass in each hand. Her black pubic hairs were frosted with his dried sperm, her breasts were large and low-hanging. "Here," she said, kneeling on the bed.

He took the glass and held it up to the neon light that flashed outside the window. The liquid was clear and brown, and in it floated two cubes of ice. He brought it to his lips, took a swig, and it burned all the way down.

The Last Buffoon

Suddenly he was struck by a sensation of utter chaos, as if the sky had fallen on his head and the world was reeling drunkenly. His consciousness

Now wait a minute, Frapkin, you fucking bum — that last sentence is a plagiarism from Yukio Mishima's great story *Patriotism*, and you damn well know it.

Gee it is, isn't it.

Don't act dumb, you lousy cockroach. You're always plagiarizing, and that's the mark of the lowlife hack that you are.

Well, I can't help it if I've got a good memory, and anyway, if a line is good it deserves wider dissemination. The people who read these crummy books deserve a good line once in a while, and I can't take the time to invent them.

That insipid rationalization reveals the true depths of your garbage-pail nature. Plagiarism is despicable and dishonorable. How can you stand yourself?

Because poverty is even worse — I've got to get this book finished so I can get some money money money. He who hesitates has to wait longer for his advance.

Shrank to a single hairlike thread of steel, and he realized that the bitch had slipped him a mickey.

"We've got you this time, Ripelli," she said.

Somehow he had to get moving, to get out of there, but he felt himself

Riinnnggggg.

"Frank McFarland at Criterion, Frapkin. Are you finished

with the new Triggerman?"

"I've got a few more days to go."

"We're moving up the publication date, but if you can get it to us in a few days, that'll be fine."

"You'll have it. By the way, when're you going to pay for the last one?"

"When you deliver this one."

"When'll I get paid for this one?"

"When you hand in the next one. Listen, what do you want to get paid for? You're having fun aren't you?"

"You're the second guy who told me that this week. What the fuck makes you think I'm having fun?"

"You mean sex and violence aren't fun?"

"I only have fun when I cash your checks."

He haw-haws. "You've got a good sense of humor, Frapkin, and guys with a good sense of humor don't need money. I'll see you in a few days." He hangs up on me yet again.

This time I won't let myself get so mad that I can't write. I'll just square off with my trusty old Royal and hit the keys.

Falling back onto the pillow. He'd eluded them for a long time, but now they had him.

He awoke bound and gagged in the trunk of a moving automobile. His head a tattoo of pain, he remembered what had happened, how the French bitch betrayed him, and realized he had to escape somehow. The Mafia bastards wouldn't play with him once they opened the trunk; this trip was a one-way ticket to a rub-out.

The Last Buffoon

A key turning in my front door. I rise and walk out of my office just as Mrs. Mabra Frapkin stumbles into the kitchen. She's carrying a suitcase, mop, broom, and shopping bag from the A&P.

"Good afternoon," she wheezes.

"Good afternoon."

"I am disturbing you?"

"Yes."

"I am so sorry, but I must clean. I cannot live like this."

"Do whatever you have to, but don't make a lot of noise. By the way, did your boyfriend give you a prescription for me?"

"Yes — here it is." She opens her raincoat and underneath is a blue chambray shirt and bib denim overalls. Reaching into a pocket, she pulls out the prescription.

I peck it from her fingers. "I'm going back to work now — please be quiet."

"I have a letter for you. It was in the mailbox downstairs."

From her pocket comes the envelope, and in the corner I reach BACCHUS PRESS. Can this possibly, through some miraculous intervention of God, be a royalty check? I grab the envelope, tear it open, and find a memo attached to a letter. This memo has the Bacchus imprint and says:

> *Dear Alex,*
> *This fan letter came in today, and I thought you'd like to see it.*
>
> *Lou*

The letter is handwritten on a pink piece of paper

85

smelling like lilacs, and says:

Dear Mr. Wimbledon,

I just read your terrific book called Patti's Honeymoon *and I liked it so much I thought I'd write to tell you so. You must be a very experienced man to know about all those things. Do you think we could meet sometime? I live in New York City, and if you ever come to town, call me at my office (537-6780) or my apartment (691-9091).*

Yours truly,
Betty Herndon

I do a fast about face, run into my office, slam the door, dive for the telephone, and dial.

"Legano Motor Transport," says a young woman.

"Betty Herndon, please." My heart is pounding like a jackhammer.

Bzzzzzzzzz.

"Mr. Legano's office."

"Betty Herndon, please."

"Speaking."

"I'm Lancelot Wimbledon — hello."

"Who?"

"I wrote a novel called *Patti's Honeymoon*, and I've just received a charming letter from you about it."

"Oh! Well, what a nice surprise. When did you get in town?"

"About twenty years ago — I live here."

"How good of you to call."

"How could I not call?"

"I thought you might be too busy."

"I'm not that busy. What are you doing tonight?"

"Nothing."

"Let's get together."

"Would you like to come up to my place?" she asks temptingly, and I slide my hand into my pants to save my swelling erection from strangulation by jockey shorts.

"Where do you live?"

"At 275 West 38th Street."

"You live in the garment district?"

"Yes — I have a loft that I'm subletting from a photographer. It's very nice.

"What would be a good time?"

"Six?"

"That's fine with me."

"I'll look forward to meeting you, Mr. Wimbledon."

"And I'll look forward to meeting you, my dear."

What an incredible stroke of luck this is! It just goes to show you that if an artist works hard and is completely dedicated, the world will respond eventually. Covering my typewriter with its vinyl coat, I unbutton my shirt and enter the living room, almost tripping over my wife on her hands and knees scrubbing the floor.

"My God — what're you doing?" I cry.

She looks up, an Yves Saint Laurent bandana around her head. I'm cleaning your filthy floor."

"Do you have to get down on your hands and knees like

that?"

"Do you have a maid?"

"No."

"Then I have to do it. If I am going to live here it must be clean."

"Aren't you going a little overboard?"

"It takes work to make clean. I do not want to catch a disease."

"If you do, I'm sure your boyfriend will cure you real fast."

"Why not go back to your office and let me do my clean."

"I have a business appointment, and I have to get ready."

I run to the bathroom, close the door, undress, and turn on the water. It's cold in here so I push down the window. The rotted bottom of the sash hits the sill, breaks apart, and falls into the bathtub, followed by the glass window, which crashes as it lands, becoming tiny jagged triangles and parallelograms. I now have an open-air bathroom. This fucking building is falling apart and naturally this had to happen at the crucial moment when I'm preparing for a great sexual experience. I wrap myself in my towel, speed barefooted out of the bathroom, cross the living room where my wife is playing scrubwoman, enter my office and dial the number of my landlord.

"Shapiro Realty," says an old broad.

"Lemme speak to Shapiro."

"Whoze callink please?"

"The Commissioner of Housing."

"One moment please."

Click clack.

"Hello," coos my landlord Shapiro, the nastiest man alive.

"This is Alexander Frapkin in apartment 22, 123 Christopher Street and — "

"My secretary said you were the Commissioner of Housing. His voice has returned to its normal gangster tone.

"That old nut's liable to say anything. I'm calling because my bathroom window just fell out and I'd like to have it fixed immediately. This is November and it's cold in there."

"Put your coat on."

"I can't take a shower with my coat on."

"Don't get smart with me, Frapkin! I know who you are — troublemaker!"

I make my voice hard as a truncheon. "If you don't have this window fixed by noon tomorrow, I'm going downtown to the Department of Housing and raise hell until they make you fix it, and you know as well as I that they're fed up with all the violations in your buildings. They're liable to drag you into court and fine you twenty thousand dollars, so what's it going to be, slumlord?"

"Someday something terrible's going to happen to you, Frapkin."

"Something terrible happened the day I moved into this building. When're you going to get somebody over here to fix my window?"

"Lemme write down the information. You say you broke the window in the bathroom?"

"I said it fell out because the wood was rotten all the way through."

"You mean it fell out all by itself? How could it fall out all by itself?"

The bastard's trying to figure a way to send me a bill. "It

89

fell out when I tried to close it. The broken glass made a two-inch gash in my hand and right now I'm bleeding profusely. I've already spoken to my lawyer and we'll probably sue."

"Will somebody be there the rest of the day?"

"I'm leaving for the hospital right now, but my wife'll be here."

"Your wife?"

"You heard me."

"You got a wife, now?"

"That's right, and if anything happens to me, she'll carry on the fight."

"She must be a *meshuginah* like you."

"She's even worse."

Shapiro takes two deep audible breaths. "I got a man working in your neighborhood. I'll send him over to your place maybe today."

"You'd better."

"Goodbye, Frapkin. Don't step into any open manholes."

"I'm living in an open manhole."

I hang up the phone and wonder how many months it'll be before he fixes the goddamned window. Oh what a miserable unrelenting life this is — hold on — I forgot that tonight I'm going to have a great sexual experience with one of my fans. On my way to the bathroom I pass my wife squeezing a sponge saturated with abominations into a bucket of water.

"Do you always run around your apartment like this?" she asks.

"The window fell out in the bathroom. The landlord said

90

he'd send somebody over in a little while, so stay home."

"I must go out to get the rest of my clothes."

"You've got to stay until seven o'clock at least. I'd stay myself but I have, as I told you, an important business engagement." I take three steps to the bathroom but remember I've got to cover the hole so I don't catch pneumonia on this crucial night, and by the way, what time is it?

I return to my office-bedroom, check my watch, and see it's about a hundred minutes to sexual intercourse. Opening a dresser drawer, I take out a fresh tan cowboy shirt, remove the rectangle of cardboard inserted by the laundry, open my tool box, select a hammer and a few nails. I carry these to the bathroom and attach the cardboard over the hole as best I can. Then I very carefully clean all the broken wood and glass out of the tub.

And now for a leisurely shower in which I shall prepare my body for the rites of love. I turn on the water, adjust temperature, and get in. warm water pours onto me from above and streams of cold air from the window stab my kidneys. While I'm in Japan I must go to one of those public baths where geisha girls wash you and clean your pipes. Maybe I should move to Japan instead of California. I could study karate and Zen, and if things ever got really bad, I could commit ritual disembowelment, and the Japanese would understand.

After the shower I shave my neck in the big magnifying mirror, noticing with dismay that I'm looking more and more like my father, and I'm turning into a crackpot like him too. I fought the old bastard from the time I could walk, but now, in death, he's taken possession of me.

Clean, shaved, cologne, and wrapped in a towel, I open the bathroom door and see my wife scrubbing years of grease, peanut butter, spilled orange juice, milk stains, dried rice kernels, and ossified roach carcasses, off the kitchen tiles. Her angelic tanned face is oily, eyes tired, lips pale. I really ought to help her, but I must help myself to some pussy.

"When will you be back?" she asks.

"I have no idea."

"I was hoping you would help me move some of my things in."

"What's wrong with your boyfriend?"

"He's on duty tonight at the hospital."

"Sorry, I guess you'll have to get one of your other boyfriends."

She looks at me angrily. "I am not a cheap American girl like the ones I am very sure you know. I do not have twenty boyfriends."

"I know you're not cheap — your boyfriend paid a thousand dollars for you today."

She stands up, puts her hands on her hips, blows hair away from her mouth. "That was a loan!"

"Sure it was."

"I know you do not believe me. You think everybody does everything for money just like you."

"That's right."

"Well I want you to know that I am not like that."

"Sure you're not."

"You are such a stupid low-class man!"

I should empty that bucket of slop over her head, but she

92

hasn't been in this country a very long distance and doesn't know any better. What time is it? I leave her standing in the kitchen and rush to the office-bedroom — it's quarter to seven. I have plenty of time. Slowly and carefully I dress in my customary clothes, puffing Colombian buds in my handy home glass hookah as I do so. I shouldn't waste my time and energy in arguments, because my life situation shows signs of improving. I have a thousand dollars, some excellent dope, an apartment in the process of being cleaned, a rendezvous with a possible sex slave, and my latest Triggerman is almost finished. If all continues well I'll have enough money soon to relax for a few months and write a serious novel. I can see the headlines on the front page of the *New York Times Book Review* now: MAJOR NEW WRITER BURSTS UPON LITERARY SCENE. I roll two joints and tuck them in the top of my Burlington no-static socks. Lastly I put on my Burberry, my Borsalino, and my French sunglasses.

My wife is scrubbing the greasy mess underneath the kitchen sink. "You are leaving now?"

"Do you think I hang around the house dressed like this?"

"I have to talk with you about something."

"I'm all ears."

"I was thinking — I will sleep on the sofa, yes?"

"You can sleep in my bed if you like."

"Where will you sleep?"

"In my bed with my arms around you."

She smiles diplomatically. "I will sleep on the sofa. Where will I put my things?"

"I don't even know where my things are, so how should I

know about your things?"

"I can hang clothes in your closet?"

"If you can find room."

"Thank you very much."

"You're welcome very much."

She goes back to scrubbing. "That is all I wanted to ask you about. I hope your business goes well."

"See you later." I slap her fondly across her lovely ass.

"I am not accustomed — "

Before she can finish I'm out the door.

• • •

West 38th Street is in the heart of the garment district, and both sides of the street are lined with trucks loading and unloading when I arrive. Puerto Ricans and blacks push racks of dresses and coats over the streets and sidewalks, and other workers are leaving the area on their way home. It is here that I shall initiate my sex slave into esoteric erotic practices. Oh Frapkin, if Masters and Johnson had only known about you.

She lives in an old five-story commercial building whose ground floor is occupied by: SAM GRUPSKY, WHOLSESALE FEATHER MERCHANT.

If his feathers weren't wholesale I'd pick up a few with which to tickle Betty's clitorini. The poor girl doesn't know what she's in for — sexual deprivation has made me even more depraved than when I wrote *Patti's Honeymoon*.

To the left of Grupsky's window display is a door which I open, entering a small vestibule. I look at the buttons and next to the one for the fifth floor is "Betty Herndon" typewritten on a little sliver of paper affixed with scotch tape.

94

The Last Buffoon

I press the button twice, wait several seconds, and press twice again. No answer. My heart sinks as I speculate that perhaps something happened and she won't make it home.

"Who is it?" asks Betty Herndon's sweet voice over the intercom.

"Lancelot Wimbledon."

"Oh, hi. I'm on the top floor." The door buzzes and I push it open. Up the stairs I go. Dirty yellow paint is peeling from the walls but I've been in loft buildings worse than this where the apartments were sensational. On the Second floor is the VENUS LINGERIE CORPORATION, surely a good omen, on the third is MANCHESTER KNITTING MILLS, the fourth is split between a hat maker and a job lot distributor, and on the fifth floor I see the door to paradise. I fly to it, knock, it opens, and standing in front of me is a wet dream come true — a Marilyn Monroe blonde with big tits, rosy cheeks, and a short dress.

"Mr. Wimbledon?" she says with a smile.

"Yes indeed."

"I'm Betty — please come in."

She turns around and displays an adorable round ass into which I soon shall ram my dick. I follow her into a corridor where large chunks of plaster are missing from the walls, and the door closes behind us. This looks like a vacant factory loft, and how did the door close behind us? I turn around and see standing there a big ugly nightmare with a beer belly and a nose like a pink turnip. Betty Herndon scampers down the corridor, and passing her coming my way is another big ugly nightmare, this one in baggy green workpants, blue bomber jacket, and battered fedora on the back of his head.

A gallon of adrenalin pours into my bloodstream. "What's going on here!"

Paloof! Right in the mouth, stunning me cold. Kaplow! On the other side of my face, and my genuine imported French sunglasses shatter against my nose. My skull feels split open, I see stars, and I fall back against the ropes, ready to go down for the count with the very next punch.

Turnip Nose and Bomber Jacket grab me by the arms and drag me into the big room. In its center is a man dressed in a suit, topcoat, and homburg. He's got a trimmed mustache and black hair going gray at the temples. He flexes his fingers inside tight black gloves.

"Hold him in the light so I can see him," he says.

"This has got to be some kind of terrible mistake," I groan through bloody lips.

"Are you Lancelot Wimbledon?"

"Yes but — "

"Did you write this book?" He pulls a worn copy of *Patti's Honeymoon* out of his coat pocket.

"Yes but — "

"You sick bastard!" He rears back his black fist, the two goons hold me tight, and his fist grows larger. Kerbamm! My chin swaps places with my forehead, my legs become macaroni. "I caught my thirteen-year-old daughter reading it!"

Bomber Jacket slaps me down, finds my wallet, takes it out, and hands it to the gentleman, who looks through my cards. "Alexander Frapkin's his name. He lives on Christopher Street in the Village. That figures." He shoots a hard right jab to my stomach, doubling me over. Rice Krispies with whole-wheat toast climb my throat.

"Open the window," he says to Betty Herndon, who's been standing in a corner.

"My God, you're not going to throw him out!"

"I said open the window."

She unhooks the latch and bends to push it up as I yell, "No!"

Pabamm! In my mouth again. A thousand and one nights fall over me. I can feel myself being lifted, pushed, kicked, and when I open my eyes I'm hanging head-down out the window!

"How do you like it out there?" asks the gentleman above me.

I can see an alley, the back of a building. Oh God, I'm going to die. Tears fill my eyes and drip into my few remaining hairs.

"I said how do you like it out there?"

I open my mouth to speak, but my throat is constricted with fear and no sound comes. Coughing to clear out, I manage a garbled scream. "I don't like it very much."

They let go of my left foot, and I catch a glimpse of my grave. "Please don't drop me!"

They release my right foot, and the grave opens wide for me, but after falling a few inches I'm caught by my left foot again. "How'd you like that one?"

"I've got a little daughter with polio and she'll be an orphan!"

"No man with a daughter would write a book like that, you filthy pervert!"

"Helllllpppppp!"

"Nobody can year you — pig!"

If I ever get out of this alive I'll go to shul every Friday night and Saturday morning. I'll become a good person and won't jerk off so much. I'll give to charity.

"Hey, cockroach!"

"What?"

"If I ever see another one of your books on the stands we'll do this again and next time we'll drop you — understand?"

"I understand."

The goons haul me up; I scrape my hands trying to hold the brick wall away from my face. As I go over the sill, buttons are torn from my Burberry coat, and I don't even know where my hat is. A man like me should carry a gun at all times.

Turnip Nose and Bomber Jacket grab me by the arm and slam me against the wall. My head bounces off it and makes a sharp hard noise. The gentleman stands in front of me and to his left rear is pale Betty Herndon. They're in a kaleidoscope that someone is turning.

"I'm not kidding, degenerate," the gentleman says. "Next time you're dead, and if you go to the police, you'll be worse than dead!"

What can be worse than being dead?

He makes a fist. Blam blam blam! I am falling.

I awaken alone on the floor of the loft, my beard wet with blood, hatchets whacking my head. I can't breathe through my nose and there are ten angry rats chewing their way out of my stomach. I appear to be alive, although to what extent I'm not quite sure.

I think I can get up, but before I do I must resolve never in my life to use my real name on a book, never answer a fan

98

letter, never permit a photograph of myself to be used anywhere, and never do any publicity whatsoever. Fear of incidents like this must be behind the paranoia of Salinger and Pynchon, of James Joyce. Faulkner said don't tell the bastards anything, and he was right. This is my own fault.

I've got to get out of here. I place my palms on the greasy floor and raise up a few inches. An axe hits my dome and the rats take huge bites out of my intestines. I pause for a few moments until the pain diminishes. Steady as she goes. I'm on my knees now, and all the way up. I'm standing next to the open window; cool zephyrs caress my aching face. That feels better. Frapkin will survive even this.

I see a sink and cracked mirror in the corner, push myself from the all, and swerve in that direction. It's an old steel tub shaped like an orange crate. I lean my thighs against it and in the fading daylight look at the mirror. Good grief — is that the Amazing Frapkin? Unless I'm looking through a hole in the wall at a bloody old derelict, it is indeed the Amazing Frapkin. Gingerly I touch my nose. Ouch! It looks straight — maybe nothing's broken. I bare my teeth and see they're rinsed with blood but all present and accounted for. If I had broken ribs I couldn't have walked over here. It appears that I'm still in one piece and relatively sound.

I'd better not hang around — those maniacs might decide to come back and finish me off. I'll bet that thirteen-year-old daughter is a hot little number. Stop thinking about that! My insatiable lust will be the ruin of me yet. Maybe God's trying to tell me something.

I turn on the faucet to wash up, but no water comes out. This isn't my day. I guess I'll have to return home like this, and I'd better get going while I'm still able. Stumbling to the doorway, I see my mangled Borsalino on the floor. I bend to pick it up and nearly black out. Steady, Frapkin, don't make fast moves. I harvest it, knock out the crown, and with the blade of my hand smack in my traditional Mafioso crease. It's smudged with filth but its shape is still perfect; there's nothing like a real Borsalino. My sunglasses are beyond salvage, I'll have to buy another pair at Sex Fifth Avenue or maybe Bazoomingdale's. I fetch my wallet and drop it into my coat pocket.

Hanging onto the bannister and wall, I hobble down the creaky stairs. Should I take a chance and report this savage beating to the cops? I'd better not, because if those brutes did what they did there's every reason to believe they'll do what they said. No cops.

I open the downstairs door and step onto the crowded sidewalk. Pedestrians glance at my bloodied face and clothes and keep walking. People like me are common sights on the sidewalks of New York. I walk into the street and hold up my hand, but two empty cabs pass me by — they don't want me to bleed or die in their back seat, and who can blame them? The closest subway is at Sixth Avenue and 42nd Street, so I lean in that direction, my head still taking whacks, a few rats still scratching in my guts. America doesn't appreciate her great hack writers — that's for sure. Like a ragged soldier in the Army of Lost Souls, I make my way to the subway.

I'm standing on the subway platform watching my train thunder into the station. The engineer hits the brakes, a million vampires scream, the train slows to a stop, the doors

100

crank open. I stumble aboard and collapse onto a bench. I think I'll close my eyes and sink into a deep state of Buddhist meditation that'll help my poor body heal itself. Wait a minute — the woman sitting opposite me looks familiar. She's tall and rawboned with a face like an owl wearing glasses. I think she's one of those lady reporters I coped with during my illustrious press agent days.

"Stop staring at me!" she screams, gnashing her teeth and making fists.

Everybody on the subway car looks at bruised and battered Alexander Frapkin, and I turtle into my coat collar. "You look like somebody I used to know."

"I couldn't possibly know anybody like you!"

I close my eyes and escape.

• • •

At the door of my apartment I'm assailed by the odor of soap, ammonia, and perfume. My wife, in a mauve bathrobe, sits on the sofa, knees in the air, heels against her ass, doing her fingernails. When she sees me she jumps up and lets out a cry.

"What happened?"

"I got mugged." I slam the door and snap all the latches.

She runs toward me and looks in my purple eyes. "How did it happen?"

"It's a long story."

She heads for the phone. "I'll call Sidney."

"Whatever you do, please don't call Sidney."

Her pretty brown eyes dart around excitedly. "But we have to do something!"

"We will do something. I'll take a shower and go to bed,

101

and you'll be quiet like a little Argentine mouse." I stagger toward the bedroom-office.

"Can I make you some coffee?"

"If I drink coffee I won't be able to sleep."

"Is there anything I can do to help you?"

I stop, turn around, and grab her shoulder. "Kiss me."

She squirms away. "Don't touch me."

I continue to the bedroom and can't help noticing that my apartment is spic and span. Maybe the cleanliness and order will help me think more clearly and improve my work. When I turn on the light over my desk, I notice that she's dusted its top and rearranged my papers and materials. "Mabra!"

"What?"

"Get in here!"

She runs in on furry pink slippers. "What is it?"

"I thought I told you to leave my desk alone!"

"I just cleaned it up for you a little."

"I'll never be able to find anything!"

"Everything is right where you put it. I just made it neat."

I want to murder her in cold blood, but my head is banging fiercely. "I'll talk to you about this tomorrow. Please leave so I can get undressed."

"I am sorry to make you upset."

I point to the door. She spins and runs away. Everything is going against me all of a sudden — my ascending star has lost its momentum and is falling into hell. Undressing, I drop my clothes in a corner, take a fresh towel from a drawer and make my way past my fretting wife to the bathroom, where I turn on the shower and notice that the window hasn't been fixed. That fucking no-good Shapiro. God, there goes my head again — I'd better think nice thoughts. I stand under the pouring water and watch my blood sacrifice drip down the drain. What have I done to deserve this?

When finished I climb out of the tub and glance in the mirror. Now I resemble my old man on the night he set fire to his girlfriend's porch, and her younger brother beat the piss out of him. Undaunted, he went on to incinerate her car, just as I shall continue to write despite this unfortunate episode. A Frapkin may be laid low, but he never surrenders.

Normal toweling produces sharp pain, so I daub myself carefully, trying not to curse, trying to think of flowers and babies. I wrap myself in the towel and proceed to the bedroom.

"You are all right?" Mabra asks as I pass her on the sofa.

"Yes."

"There is something I can do?"

"Come to bed and kiss me all over."

She looks exasperated. "You should get married, I think so."

"I happen to be married to you."

"I mean to a real wife."

"You are my real wife."

I limp to the bedroom, shut the door, put out the light, and fall onto my king-sized used waterbed. The ocean slogs and rocks me to sweet sleep.

CHAPTER
SEVEN

AT TWO IN THE MORNING I have to take a piss. Aching everywhere, I roll off my waterbed, put on my thonged sandals and gray hospital bathrobe, tippy-toe to the door, and open it silently, for I don't want to disturb my little wife.

I enter the living room and see her sleeping tummy-own on the sofa, moonlight streaming through the window onto the lower half of her body. She's thrown off her covers and her nightgown has risen high on the leg closest me, revealing its beautiful strong shape and the bottom of white underpants. The palms of her hands are on the pillow, her face turned away and covered by a profusion of black hair.

In the bright moonlight the scene is enchanted. Gingerly I sit on the old leather chair facing the sofa and feast my sleepy blackened eyes upon my wife as she slumbers, air sighing in and out her mouth and nose.

Is my little Argentine gypsy dreaming of Dr. Sidney Siegel striding across the heavens in his white coat and stethoscope necklace, or perhaps of the pampas at midday, horses grazing on yellow grass? Might she be wrestling with an old goat, symbolic of her new husband, or is the Lord telling her she shouldn't have violated the marriage sacrament for a paltry green card?

It's strange, but my desire isn't specifically sexual. I want to do more than merely hold her in my arms and stick in my cock. I want to dissolve my entire body into hers, mix my blood with hers, unite with her beauty, and become beautiful myself.

My bladder distracts me. Arising quietly, I pass through the darkness to the bathroom, turn on the light that momentarily blinds me, and close the door. Taking out Charlie, I piss into the bowl. There are no traces of blood in my urine; I appear to have survived the vicious beating with no more than superficial bruises and pains. Five hundred years ago they burned people like me at the stake, but now they only beat us up once in awhile. Things are getting better all the time.

On the way to bed I'm halted once more by the sight of Mabra in dreamland. She's moved into the fetal position with her bare kneecaps toward me and her face still hidden by the tangled net of her hair. She's sort of loveable with her mops and brooms and Latin bullshit; her beauty surely indicates merit won in past lives. Sleep well, my princess of the pampas.

Silently in the moonlight I bow and gently touch my lips to her hair.

The car turned onto a rough country road. In the trunk, Ripelli gripped the tire iron in his right hand. He didn't know how many of them were in the car, but he was ready. If he got out of this one he'd track down that French broad and strangle her with his bare hands.

The car continued for another mile, then turned to the right and stopped. Ripelli moved himself into a position where he could swing the tire iron soon as the trunk opened. He heard them talking, heard them get out of the car and walk back toward him.

"We'll just dump him over the cliff here," one of them said.

They shuffled around and a key scraped into the trunk lock. Ripelli saw a shaft of moonlight and a man with a nose like a turnip lifting the lid. Behind him was a hoodlum in a blue jacket and a dapper guy in a homburg, all with guns at the ready.

Ripelli swung the tire iron with all his might at the hoodlum opening the trunk. The nub of the iron caught him in the eye, crushing it and cracking his cheekbone. He fell back screaming horribly, and Ripelli bounded out of the trunk, got set, and thrust the sharp end of the tire iron six inches into the fat stomach of the hoodlum in the blue jacket. Blood gushed out, the hoodlum's eyes rolled into his head, and Ripelli snatched away his gun and used his body as a shield against the bullets being fired in wild panic by the dapper guy in the homburg.

Ripelli took aim around the sagging bleeding twitching body and fired two rounds at the dapper man. The first blew apart his mustache and most of his face, the second made a big dark splotch on the collar of his white shirt. Ripelli fired again and

Rrriiiiinnnnngggggggg.

"Hello?"

"This is Jake — haven't you forgot something?"

"Oh yeah. I was supposed to pay you some money a few

days ago."

"You haven't got it?"

"Of course I've got it, but I had an accident and I've been staying home in an effort to recuperate."

"What kinda accident?"

"I fell down a flight of stairs."

"You're not tryin' to con an old con man, are you?"

"You'll be able to see with your own eyes. Do you want me to bring the money over right now?"

"If you can get up out of your sick bed."

"I'll have to go to the bank first. Can I see you in about an hour?"

"I'm having a little scene over here, so you might want to bring a bottle of something."

"Any broads there?"

"Would I have a scene without broads?"

I hang up the phone and realize I should stay home and finish today's fifteen pages before going to Jake's, but a debt is a debt and should be discharged as soon as possible, and I'm three days late as it is. What shall I wear, my normal uniform being torn and filthy due to my date with Betty Herndon? I look through the closet, now smelling of Mabra's fragrant clothes jammed in with mine, and see my choice is between blue jeans or press agent clothes. I'm too old to walk around like a hippie, so it'll have to be a press agent outfit. If William Burroughs can wear suits all the time, so can I.

But which suit? There's my glen plaid, the brown herringbone, the basic blue, the blazer and gray pants combination, the houndstooth number, and my stunning movie premiere tuxedo which of course is out of the question. I think the basic blue might be the best all-round selection since its styling is least out-of-date, and I'll match it with a light blue shirt and maroon tie. Over everything shall drape my black Joe College raincoat lined with zipout golden fleece, and on my head shall sit my genuine gray Irish wool floppy-brimmed hat, Secret Agent Frapkin's favorite back-up hat. I'll look like a respectable but somewhat eccentric gentleman, and might even be invited to join the local Chamber of Commerce, where I shall plant a bomb.

I dress quickly, feeling the pangs of my old press agent responsibility as I don the garments. Putting the Alvin Jones check in my breast pocket, I gather together what must go to the cleaners, and walk into the living room, where my little wife has set up her ironing board and is doing a blouse.

"I have a business appointment," I tell her. "If there are any calls for me, write down the person's name, the time he called, and the message if any."

She looks up from her ironing, is wearing jeans and a sweater. "I have to go to a job interview today, so I won't be home much longer."

"What kind of job interview?"

"At New York University Hospital?"

"To do what?"

"To be a nurses' aide."

"Are you kidding me?"

"No."

"Nurses' aides empty bedpans and bathe people who're dying. Is that what you want to do?"

"I have to make some money."

"Why don't you smarten up and make Dr. Siegel take care of you?"

Her iron makes fast erratic movements. "I am not that kind of woman, and I do not want to talk with you about it because I do not want to have an argument."

"If you have to work, why don't you get a job in a fancy boutique on the East Side? You've got class — you shouldn't be carrying bedpans full of shit around."

"Thank you very much for your advice."

"I can get you a job as a topless dancer, if you want."

"A what?"

"You know — you take off all your clothes and dance on top of a bar."

"Are you crazy!"

"It pays very well."

"No!"

"I was just trying to be helpful."

"Please don't give me your helpful."

I look at my watch. "I'd better get going."

"I hope your business goes very well."

"Thank you, and happy bedpans." I slap her ass and run for the door.

"Keep your hands away from me, you stupid crazy!"

Hurtling down the stairs, I nearly fall onto Mary, the old Italian lady who lives alone in the apartment directly beneath me, and who likes to take walks in the dark hallway. She's wearing a dirty black dress, puffs a cigarette, looks like a retired witch who eats too much. "How're you doin', Frapkin?" she asks in a crackly voice.

Evidently her vision is bad and she can't see my face too

well. "I'm okay. How about you?"

"So-so. You gotta goil livin' witcha up there?"

"I got married again."

She wrinkles her forehead and turns down the corners of her mouth. "Again?"

"That's right."

"You ain't gotta lie to me — I know young people live together these days without getting' married. You think I'd get married if I was young today? What for? Look at Mrs. Castelango on the third floor — her husband gets drunk and beats her up, and she stays with him because the priest says she's gotta. If I was her I'd tell the priest to go to hell, wait until my husband falls asleep, pour a little lighter fluid on him, and make a bonfire. Why should anybody be stuck with the same person for the rest of her life?"

It never takes much to get her going. "I've got to get to the bank before it closes. Speak to you later, Mary."

"Yeah." She raises her cigarette to her mouth.

Down the stairs and out the front door I go. The sun is a silver ball behind the blanket of clouds, and the sidewalk is loaded with cowboys. You expect to see a stagecoach come thundering by, followed by a gang of bandits, but then you realize that Christopher Street cowboys wear eye shadow and reek of cologne, this being fag alley, not Abilene.

However I'm not anti-faggot — don't get me wrong. No one should be barred from any job on account of sexual habits. If a man wants to get fucked in the ass, that's his business. But I wish these looney bastards would find another neighborhood to hang out in because they're driving me nuts.

My first stop is the dry cleaners, where I must make

arrangements to have my clothing repaired and cleaned, and my Borsalino blocked.

"Vhat happened to you?" asked the dry cleaner.

"I tripped and fell."

"You musta fell down a mountain. You sure some guy didn't catch you in bed mit his vife?"

"I should be so lucky."

He takes the clothes and gives me a little slip of paper, which I put into my wallet. Next I stroll to the Chemical Bank on Sheridan Square, where I maintain a perpetually troubled special checking account. Pushing through two bulletproof glass doors, I enter the great hall of money, money, money.

An old guard who couldn't shoot his way out of a pastrami sandwich looks at me suspiciously although he's seen me here a thousand times and should know by now that I'm harmless, although I'm not. As an authority on criminology, I think this bank could be knocked over quite easily. Often I've thought of getting together with a few desperados and trying it, but with my luck that senile guard would try to be a hero, take a wild shot, and score a direct hit on my foolish heart.

In front of the tellers are lines of Villagers, many of them common businessmen masquerading as bohemians, the phony bastards. The one good thing you can say about the Rockefellers is that they don't pretend to be artists.

I endorse Charles Jones' check, fill out a deposit slip for seven hundred dollars, and get in the line formed before the prettiest teller, a saucy little brunette who looks like a playboy bunny. She's working in a fog as usual, and whenever she has to check the files, walks like it's her last mile. Her eyes are half-closed and she's obviously been fucking and sucking all night, which is infuriating because she hasn't been fucking and sucking me. Her clothes are rumpled, meaning she hasn't even been home yet, the little bitch. I'd give my left ball for an hour alone with her, but she's the type who goes for flashy young guys. When she's about twenty-seven and completely fucked out she'll marry a bigshot bank executive, then spend the rest of her life as a Westchester matron, raising a brood of tennis players and her eyebrows should anyone tell an off-color joke.

I wait patiently in line making goo-goo eyes at all the good-looking women, none of whom respond, as usual, and finally it's my turn before the little tart. I pass her my papers, she studies them with bloodshot eyes, then shuffles to the counter to check the books, returns, stamps my deposit slip, gives me three hundred dollars in cash and a receipt, and I try to convince her through ESP to spend her next sleepless night with me, but she doesn't even look at me once, and another ESP experiment has failed.

I stop at the neighborhood drugstore and drop off Dr. Sidney Siegel's prescription, then go to the nearest liquor store for a bottle of Ouzo, which I know Jake likes and will complement the variety of chemicals I expect him to have at his scene.

• • •

Jake opens the door and looks at my face. "Who beat you up?" He's wearing baggy chino pants and a checkered shirt hanging over his fat gut.

"I fell down a flight of stairs."

112

The Last Buffoon

"I don't believe it."

"I don't care what you believe."

He smiles diabolically. "Your new wife go after you with her rolling pin?"

"Don't be ridiculous."

"You fuck her yet?"

"No."

"Schmuck."

"I've got a thousand dollars out of the deal so far, so I'm not such a schmuck." Reaching into my pocket, I come out with a fistful of cabbage. "I owe you a hundred, right?"

"Right."

I count it out and slap it onto his hand. "There you go. I always pay my debts."

He recounts the money and stuff it into his pocket. "At least you have so far."

I hand him the bottle in the brown bag. "Here."

He pulls it out, inspects the label, and smiles. "Thanks, baby."

I take off my hat and coat, hanging them up in the closet.

"How come you're all dressed up?" he asks.

"No special reason."

I follow him into the living room, wishing I had a new pair of sunglasses to conceal my eyes from his guests, half of whom I don't know. He introduces me around and I smile and nod, shake a few hands, but my eyes are repeatedly drawn to his little round coffee table on which sit two different kinds of marijuana, a block of medium-brown hashish, some yellow pills, and two mounds of white powder which must be cocaine and heroin. The stereo is turned to disco music, loud

113

enough to hear the words but not sufficient to prohibit conversation. It's going to be a loverly afternoon.

"Siddown and help yourself," Jake says, "but I warn you, if you get freaky I'm gonna throw you out."

He takes the Ouzo to the kitchen while I sit on the middle of the sofa beside one of the Village's great insane beauties, Nikki Aranopoulis, who hit town about ten years ago from Pittsburg, which for some strange reason has produced a lot of nuts. She's got straight black hair, a thin nose, Mona Lisa lips, and is a bit overweight, which makes her look soft and sexy. She's dressed in black and adorned with antique jewelry.

"Whataya say, Nikki."

"Hello, Frapkin." She's staring into space and looks content as a billionaire.

I bend over the goodies on the table. "What do you recommend?"

"The schmeck."

It's white powder in a red plastic bowl. I spoon some up, snort it in, and fall into a truckload of marshmallows. For a few seconds I feel mildly nauseous, then become cozy and warm.

Plunking down on the other side of me is Becky Rabinowitz, chubby, neckless, with long honey-blonde hair and eyeglasses. She's a physicist who does top-secret rocket research for the government in New Jersey someplace. Breaking off some hash with chewed-up fingernails, she puts little lumps in a rosewood pipe, applies a flame, and huffs and puffs.

She fidgets, lays the pipe on the table, wiggles her ass, and turns to me with a big toothy grin, because she's been in love with me for years.

"How've you been, Frapkin?"

"Pretty good."

"Jake told me somebody beat you up."

"I didn't get beat up — I fell down a flight of stairs."

"You can't get black eyes falling down a flight of stairs. Jake told me your new wife did it to you."

"That's a lie."

"Are you really married again?"

"Yes."

"For money?"

"Of course."

"You know — some people actually get married because they like each other."

"So I've heard."

"Maybe you should try it."

"I don't have time for foolishness."

I get up, stagger across the room, and drop into the chair next to an old guy who looks like a WASP college professor down on his luck. He's talking to a black cat in a white turtleneck sweater, Jake's coke connection.

"The land belongs to the Palestinians," the professor says. "Israel should give it back."

I've got to get away from this guy before I kill him. Pushing myself erect, I nearly keel over on my face, but manage to catch myself and stumble toward the Ouzo.

I enter Jake's cubbyhole kitchen. On the counter are uneven ranks of bottles, and a bag of ice is in the sink. Leaning against the refrigerator is Al the bartender from Lucky's on Barrow Street, talking to Dave the chiropractor.

They interrupt their conversation to say hello, then continue as I pour myself a shot.

"The fucking unions are ruining the country," says Al the bartender. "Why should a fucking garbage collector make twelve thousand dollars a year?"

"The city's broke because of the unions," replies Dave the chiropractor, who's wearing a Beethoven T-shirt.

I want to throw the bottle of Ouzo at the fucking fascists. Holding my glass tightly, I carry it into the living room and sit alone on the floor in a corner, so I can drink in peace — away from crazy Becky, ant-Semites, and dopes who blame the collapse of the economy on poor working stiffs instead of robber barons.

Stupid people piss me off. Maybe I should smoke a joint and go home before I make a scene. I'd stick around if there were some pretty girls, but Nikki's the only one and she's shot me down so many times I feel like the Luftwaffe. Gulping Ouzo, I stand and make my way to the coffee table, where I kneel as if before an altar.

Nikki is a statue on one end of the sofa, and two women are talking next to her. I find the cigarette papers and roll a joint out of grass that looks like the Chicago Light Green that was so popular a few years ago. Lighting it, I inhale and hold my breath. My nose turns into a corkscrew and my ears become Chinese fans.

"Oppression must be countered by the armed resistance of women everywhere," says one of the women on the sofa. She's got a rocky face, short black hair, and a mean little mouth.

"The time has come for the establishment of an Amazon empire in America," replies the other, a six-foot scarecrow.

I close my eyes and try to become tranquil, but can't. a

116

The Last Buffoon

person can take just so much. "Are you fucking insane?" I scream, standing with a smoking joint in one hand and glass of Ouzo in the other.

They look at me and press their backs against the sofa.

I'm teetering at the edge of the table, completely out of control. "Extremists in the Women's Liberation Movement are a threat to civilization!" I cry. "They preach hatred and divisiveness! They're against fucking! They're opposed to the pornographic arts! The woman governor of Connecticut vetoed a bill that would've liberalized drug laws! Down with extremists in the Women's Liberation Movement!"

Rockface stares at me. "I don't know who you are, but I think you're an idiot."

"Well I don't know who you are either, but I know what you need!" I stick the joint in my mouth, unzip my fly, and whip out my hairy canary. "This!"

The two militant women gasp. Jake puts his hand on my shoulder. "Hey, man — cool it or get out."

I turn around, cock dangling in the breeze. "What makes you think I want to stay here. What kind of party is this supposed to be! How come you didn't invite Benny the Dip, or Harry from Canarsie, or Lulu the belly dancer, or Good Time Marty? You're becoming so goddamn bourgeois it makes me sick to my stomach! Somebody ought to run a subway train over your ass!"

I stuff my member into my pants, zip up, storm to the vestibule, put on my coat and hat, and with an insolent backward glance, slam the door behind me.

117

CHAPTER EIGHT

RIPELLI CAME CRASHING through the skylight, and before his feet hit the floor his submachine gun was firing. The first burst caught Don Salvatore Castelango in the neck and severed the Mafia chieftain's head from his body. Castelango slumped forward, his neck gushing gallons of gore, and Ripelli turned, raking Nick Bombasino and Joe Lujana across the guts. They both went flying backwards, blood spurting from their torsos.

Now only Ripelli and Cecille were left standing in Castelango's office. The pretty hooker had the palms of her hands against her ashen face. "Please don't shoot me," she begged pathetically.

Ripelli pulled his trigger and the room reverberated with machine gun fire. Cecille clutched the red holes in her white dress and dropped to her knees, spitting blood. Her glazing eyes focused on Ripelli.

"How could you?" she asked.

"It was easy."

She fell onto her face and lay still, a pool of blood forming around her.

118

The Last Buffoon

Ripelli reached into his pocket and took out his calling card, which he dropped on her ass. It showed a black embossed submachine gun against a white background.

He walked down the carpeted corridor to the rear door of the Castelango mansion, where he'd parked his Ferrari Daytona. He got in, turned on the ignition, and the powerful V-12 engine roared to life. He stomped on the gas pedal and the sleek car sprang out of the driveway.

He headed for the highway out of town. He didn't know where to go next but he never thought too far ahead because he never knew when the bullet with his name on it would come along.

But he knew that somewhere, in another metropolitan cesspool, there'd be more Mafia pigs preying on innocent people, and he'd track them down and kill them just as he had in Miami.

Somebody had to.

THE END

Ladies and jellybeans, the Amazing Frapkin just completed his fifteenth, yes his *fifteenth* novel! Elated, I jump up from my desk, scream like a maniac, do a war dance atop my waterbed, open the window, and take deep draughts of sooty New York air. Whenever I finish a book I feel like Hercules after one of his labors. This one's only a Mafia melodrama but it's another link in the evidentiary chain that one day will prove me America's greatest living novelist!

Oh, I know there'll be those who'll see this book and sneer, but they couldn't write one like it if their lives depended on it. Yet I, the heroic but unsung Amazing Frapkin, have written not one but fifteen, and numerous unpublished short stories as well. One day when I'm dead Hollywood'll make a movie out of my life and call it *The Alexander Frapkin Story*, and audiences will weep over the years I toiled in poverty and obscurity. Ah, Frapkin, when the world finds out about you they'll shit their pants.

I return to my desk and call McFarland.

"This is Frapkin and I've just finished Triggerman Number Six. Have you got my check ready for Number Five?"

"It's on my desk."

"I'll be right there."

I explode out of my office into the living room, and smell my wife's perfume, the only trace of her because she hasn't come home for four nights in a row, the adulterous bitch. Wait until I'm rich and famous. She'll fall at my feet with all the rest of them, and I'll kick her ass and send her back to Dr. Sidney Siegel. Those who spurn me now will regret it when I hit the big time.

I wash and trim my beard in the bathroom, noticing Shapiro still hasn't fixed the window. Now that I'm finished with *Miami Massacre* I'll have plenty of time to straight that motherfucker out. Alexander Frapkin is nobody to trifle with.

Returning to my office, I dress in my basic blue suit ensemble, put the manuscript in my old battered pigskin briefcase, and look at myself in the mirror. Except for the beard and a certain wilted look, I'm almost like I was in the old days when I was the sharpest thing going. Was? Hell — I'm still the sharpest thing going. I've just changed my act a little.

• • •

The offices of Criterion Publications occupy the tenth floor of an old skyscraper on Seventh Avenue near 57th Street, not far from Carnegie Hall. I ride up a squeaky elevator loaded with execs looking apprehensively out the corners of their eyes at the dashing fellow in beard and floppy-brimmed Irish hat.

The elevator stops, the doors roll open, and I step into a small yellow waiting room with a counter behind which sits a pretty young girl who looks like a Sunday School teacher. I don't remove my hat because I don't want her to see my bald head.

"My name's Alexander Frapkin and Mr. McFarland is waiting to see me."

"Just a sec."

She speaks into her mouthpiece and I lean on the counter, looking at the display on the wall behind her of upcoming Criterion publications, one of which is my last Triggerman, *Hit Man Holocaust*, which shows Johnny Ripelli machine-gunning about twenty men and women.

"He'll be right out," says the Sunday School teacher.

"What's a nice girl like you doing in a place like this?"

She smiles coyly, her switchboard buzzes, she presses a button and says, "Criterion Publishing Corporation — good afternoon."

The door opens at stage left and McFarland appears, holding out his right hand. He looks like a big red-headed Irish cop and is smiling as if he's about to bust me for possession.

"Hello, Alex," he says in his musical con-artist voice.

"Hi, Frank." I shake his meaty hand.

"Come back to my office."

"Sure."

The corridor is yellow like the waiting room, and smells like ink and office machine grease. Well-dressed young executives and secretaries bustle back and forth, and in small offices they move pieces of paper and pretend to think. We pass a Xerox machine operated by a stout woman, and beyond is McFarland's office.

"Have a seat," he says, pointing to the chair beside his desk. He dresses Ivy League and looks classy, but I know from long unhappy experience how rotten he can be.

I sit and lean my attaché case against the leg of the chair. He makes himself comfortable behind his big desk. "How've you been?"

"Terrible."

"What's wrong?"

"I'm broke."

"You're always talking poormouth, but I'll bet you've got half a million dollars salted away someplace. Let's see the new Triggerman."

"Let's see the new check."

"It's in the boss's office. He hasn't signed it yet."

"I thought you said you had it on your desk."

"I did, but it wasn't signed."

"No check, no Triggerman."

He looks at the ceiling, opens his mouth, and laughs.

"Laugh all you want, but no check, no Triggerman."

"Okay, okay." His smile fading, he picks up his phone, dials four numbers, mumbles, then hangs up. "It'll take a few more minutes. Let's talk about the next one — do you have any ideas for it yet?"

"There won't be another one until you pay all the back

royalties and everything else you owe me."

"What're you talking about?"

"I'm talking about the advance for the last one, the advance for this one, and the royalties you owe me on the seven other books of mine you've already published. And please don't give me any bullshit about how if you owed me the money you would've paid me, because I've heard that song before. I want what you owe me or I'll take Triggerman someplace else."

His eyes become the splits of a tank turret. "You take Triggerman someplace else and we'll take you to court. Read your contract sometime."

"My lawyer already has, and he said he'd love to get you bastards before a judge."

"Why are you so hostile all of a sudden, Frapkin?"

"Your company has cheated me out of thousands of dollars and I want it."

He plays with a pen and looks contemplative. "Well, maybe we're so big and deal with so many authors that sometimes we lose the personal touch." He places his palms on his desk and pushes himself up. "I'm going to talk with the president of this company about you right now. I don't care what he's doing or who he's got in there — I'm going to talk to him about your situation. Just stay put and I'll be back in a few minutes."

He takes giant steps out of his office and shuts the door behind him, leaving me alone to congratulate myself on my bold power play that seems to be working. You've got to have audacity when you deal with scum. The only thing they understand is a cold-blooded threat and the determination to carry it out.

Presently the door opens and McFarland stands there like the Sergeant of the Guards. "The president would like to speak with you."

I follow McFarland down the long narrow corridor and hear choruses singing *Hail to the Chief, God Save the Queen,* and *Deutschland Uber Alles.* Editors, clerks, and secretaries look at us as we march past their offices. The president of this great American corporation is actually going to permit me a consultation in his holy of holies.

McFarland opens the door and motions for me to enter. I strut into a large rectangular office that has Picasso, Chagall, and Calder lithographs on the walls, and at one end a desk where sits an overweight man in black sideburns, green shirt, yellow tie, and coarse face. As I draw closer I see sharp canine teeth. This guy could steal your socks without taking your shoes off, stick a knife in your gut while asking how your kids are, and tell you straight-faced that black is white, up is down, and he isn't a crook.

McFarland closed the door and runs forward to make introductions. "Alex, this is Joe Greenberg. Joe, this is one of our best authors, Alex Frapkin, the creator and author of the Triggerman series."

Joe stands behind his desk and extends his hand. His sleeves are rolled up and his top shirt button undone, signifying he's a hard-working no bullshit captain of industry. "Hello, Alex."

"Hiya, Joe."

"Have a seat."

I take off my hat and sit on an upholstered green leather

chair in front of him, while McFarland drops on a chair to the right.

Joe snuggles into his seat, rests his elbows on his desk, and folds his hands in front of his chin. "What's the problem, Alex?"

I point my thumb at McFarland. "You mean he didn't tell you?"

"He told me a little, but I want to hear it straight from you."

"You owe me a lot of money."

"What do you mean — we owe you a lot of money?"

"You owe me fifteen hundred dollars for the last Triggerman, fifteen hundred for the ones I have here and maybe ten thousand in royalties on my other books. I'm not writing another word until you pay me everything."

Joe closes his eyes, shakes his head, looks exasperated. "Alex, I've got a big problem in this company," he says confidentially. "It's the chief accountant, who's a very strange person. He pays the rent, he pays the salaries, he pays the printers, he pays the distributors, but for some reason I've never been able to fathom, he doesn't like to pay the authors." He holds both hands out to me. "I'm the president of this company, Alex, and even I can't make him pay the authors." He picks up a stack of contracts and waves them at me. "We owe advances to all these authors and I can't him write out the checks — can you believe it?"

"Of course I can't believe it."

"I can't believe it either, but it's true."

"Why don't you fire him?"

"He's my brother-in-law."

"Fire him anyway."

125

"How can I fire my brother-in-law?"

"I don't know, but I'm not writing another word for Criterion until you pay me every penny you owe. I've already discussed this whole thing with my lawyer, who happens to be a former judge, and he's waiting for me to give him the green light to sue not only for monies owed but for damages as well, because lack of money is ruining my health."

Irv looks at McFarland. "How many books of Alex's have we published?"

"Four Triggermans and about three in other series."

Joe looks back at me. "After all those books you'd leave us, Alex?"

"You'd better believe it."

He sighs. "To tell you the truth, I don't blame you. I wish I had an argument but I don't because you're right, completely right, there are no two ways about it — you're right. What can I do to keep you with us?"

"Pay me."

He opens the top middle drawer of his desk and pulls out a check. "This is for the last Triggerman. I promise you I'll pay you for the new Triggerman within thirty days, out of my own private checking account if necessary, and I'll order one of my junior accountants to get to work right away figuring out your royalties so we can get completely straight with you. He'll have to do it on the sly so the chief accountant doesn't find out, but it'll be done — I promise you." He hands me the check.

I take it, make sure the numbers are right, and slide it into the inner breast pocket of my herringbone, next to my heart.

126

"Now don't you think that shows good faith, Alex?"

"It's a good start." I open my attaché case and hand him the manuscript for *Miami Massacre*. "That shows my good faith."

He lays it on his desk. "You'll do another Triggerman for us?"

"I'll tell you in thirty days."

Back on the street, I'm as jaunty as a motherfucker, with that big fat check in my breast pocket. It'll pay the rent and keep me in food long enough to finish my big novel, and then of course the millions will start pouring in.

Amid the crowds on West 57th Street, I take out the check and look at the beautiful red numerals. It's drawn on the Chase Manhattan bank two blocks away but instead of going over there and cashing it, I'll simply deposit it in the branch of my own bank two blocks the other way.

As I walk toward the bank, I feel confident and powerful. It's amazing what money can do for one's state of mind, particularly when the one in question is none other than me. People who've been economically comfortable all their lives have no concept whatever of how destructive poverty can be. Poverty has made me into the nasty character I am today. I'd much rather be sweet and light, believe me, but how can I be sweet and light in this jungle where my only protection against the ravenous capitalist class is the money that I don't have?

CHAPTER NINE

I'M IN MY OFFICE going through my notes trying to figure out what to write next, when suddenly I remember *Patti's Honeymoon*. I'd better call my English pal Geoffrey Ames right away to find out how the film project is going.

"I'm very busy right now, Alex," Geoffrey says, "What's on your mind?"

"When're you going to start filming *Patti's Honeymoon*?"

"We decided it'd be too expensive to make."

"It wouldn't be any more expensive than any other dirty movie."

"We'd need a whole resort hotel."

"In the off season you could rent one for a song."

"It'd still cost too much. If you can't make these films cheaply you can't get your money back."

"This is going to be a fantastic success — what're you talking about?"

"Nobody'll invest in a hard-core porno with a high budget."

The Last Buffoon

"You've got to sell them on the idea that this isn't just another porno film. It's *the* porno film."

"Come on, Alex — it's just another dirty story."

"Fuck you and goodbye."

Crestfallen, I hang up the phone. That porno film is a great idea and I don't care what anybody says, least of all Geoffrey. The British Empire has shrunk to a miserable damp little island because of people like him. I'll put this one together myself.

All I need are some pornographic actors and actresses, who are a dime a dozen, some equipment that I can rent, some technical people that I can hire, a script that I'll write, a resort hotel that I can borrow for a few days, and some money that I don't have.

The obstacles are the resort hotel and the money, but maybe I can convince a hotel owner to lend me his hotel in exchange for a piece of the film. He'll probably ask for a big piece, but there'll be plenty of money for everybody once it gets into general release. Okay, that leaves about fifty thousand dollars that I have to raise. Wait a minute! When I was in college I worked as a waiter one summer in a Catskills hotel owned by the Weitz family, who are best known for the chain of movie theatres bearing their name, and a few of them are on 42nd Street. All I have to do is go up to the big man's office, lay my very strong proposition on him, and let him put up the money and his hotel. How can he turn it down, particularly since he can book the film into his own theatres and really clean up? What a great benefit it is for a writer to have been a press agent, because an ordinary writer would never know how to scheme like this.

129

I dial my old office and ask for my former secretary, Ethel.

"Hello, Ethel, this is Alexander Frapkin and although I left the office eight years ago I still consider you my secretary and there's something I want you to do."

"Well hello, stranger," she says. "How've you been?"

"Pretty good. Listen, look in one of those theatre directories and tell me where the home office of the Weitz Theatre chain is, and who's their top man.

"Justa minute."

I sit and wait, planning my attack on Mister Big whoever he is.

"Alex?"

"I'm here."

"They're at 1501 Broadway, the old Paramount Building. The president is Seymour Weitz."

"Thanks, sweetheart."

"Why don't you come up sometime and say hello?"

"I'm busy."

"I've read some of your books. I had no idea you were so talented."

"What a nice thing to say."

"How come you never sent me any autographed copies?"

"I'll send you the next one. Listen, I've got to get going. Thanks for the information, and keep up the faith."

I remain at my desk a few more moments and concoct a film budget that surely will impress Seymour Weitz with my sound business mind. Dropping the presentation into my attaché case, I dress in my very fine gray pinstripe suit, back-up hat, and raincoat. I leave my humble home and take the subway uptown.

I'm approaching the old Paramount Building where the young Frank Sinatra knocked 'em dead thirty years ago. The theatre section is gone forever, renovated into offices, a bank, an Off-Track Betting parlor, and one of those Times Square gadget shops always having a going-out-of-business sale. The demise of the old Paramount Theatre is another sign of the decline of western civilization and will be duly noted as such by future historians.

In the building's lobby I peruse the register and see that Weitz Theatres, Inc. is on the fourteenth floor. I get on the elevator with a bunch of office workers and try to project the dignified knowledgeable air of Henry Kissinger. The doors close, the elevator elevates, and my guts stretch down to my knees. The elevator stops a few floors up, and my guts slam against the top of my head. It stops four more times before reaching my floor and by then I'm ready for the Emergency Vomit Team from Mount Sinai Hospital, but a girl behind a desk smiles at me and I pull myself together.

"May I help you?" she asks.

"Can you direct me to Seymour Weitz's office, please?"

"Do you have an appointment?"

"Not exactly."

She picks up the phone. "Your name please?"

"I'll just walk back — it's okay." I head for the nearest corridor.

You can't go back there like that!"

But I already have and am penetrating deeply into the Weitz fortifications. Straight ahead is a bright young executive having a drink at a water fountain.

"Can you direct me to Seymour Weitz's office please?"

He smiles, defers, thinks I'm a big shot. "Take your first left and your next left and it's at the end of the hall."

"Thank you so much."

I unbutton my Joe College topcoat and speed along, my chin thrust forward with determination, my eyes ablaze with confidence. Seymour Weitz will be unable to resist my barrage of sound business arguments, and soon I'll be rich and he'll be richer.

I hear a shuffle of footsteps behind me. "Hey you!"

Turning around, I see some guys in shirts and ties coming after me. I've got to reach Seymour before they waylay me; obviously they've been alerted by the receptionist. I break into a sprint, turn left at the first corner, left at the second, and ahead at the end of the corridor is a desk, a file cabinet, and the door. Behind the file cabinet I see the bleached blonde head of a woman trying to hide — she's been warned too.

"You can't go in there," she says weakly as I pounce on the doorknob.

I twist the big brass handle and nothing happens — they've locked the fucking thing. Turning around, I see the herd of executives bearing down on me, their ties flying in their wake. I'm trapped like a rat but I'm a smart sonofabitch and I'll merely talk my way into Weitz's office.

They stop about eight feet away, look at me, look at their leader.

He's a thickset guy with fat lips and a head round as a bowling ball. He holds out both his arms and his troops

132

form a skirmish line.

I smile at them. "Listen, I've got something very important that I've got to speak to Mr. Weitz about, and I'm sure he'll be interested because there's a lot of money in it for your company."

"He might have a gun," one of the executives says.

I smile even wider. "Don't be silly. I'm a businessman just like you. I told you that I have to speak with Mr. Weitz because…"

"Get him!"

They all dive at the same time and I'm pressed against the door by a half-ton of squirming bodies. They grab my hands and feel, pull, and I'm hanging like a monkey, looking up at hostile faces.

"Hey, whataya think this is? You can't treat me this way!"

One of them snatches my attaché case.

"Be careful," their leader says, "there might be a bomb in there."

A young executive opens my attaché case and makes a face. "There's only papers."

"When Weitz finds out about this he'll fire the whole bunch of you."

"You think we should call the cops, Bob?"

"Just throw the bum out."

"Bum! I'm going to see my lawyer and have you arrested for assault and battery!"

Bob looks down at me. "Mister, how'd you like to go to Bellevue this afternoon?"

"I don't want to go to Bellevue."

"Then shut up." He stands erect. "Let's go."

133

They carry me toward the elevator while other executives and their secretaries look from doorways and mock me, as I hang ignominiously. Beside the receptionist's desk, Bob presses the elevator button. I look sideways at the receptionist and she glowers at me with undisguised contempt.

"You people are making a terrible mistake," I say with as much dignity as I can summon.

They don't reply, hold me tight. The elevator comes, the doors open, and Bob asks the people onboard to step to the side. They do and I'm launched into the air, fly to the back wall, hit, and slide down to the floor. My attaché case lands on my lap.

"If we ever see you up here again," Bob says, "We'll press charges."

The door closes and the elevator drops. The other passengers look down at me, and I look up at them.

Maybe I'd better give up on this movie.

CHAPTER TEN

I LIMP OUT of the Paramount Building and head for the subway. Von Clausewitz said that the most important quality for field command is the ability to keep a cool head and make rational decisions in the face of the most terrible reversals, and that's what I'm trying to do right now.

The problem with this world is there are too many people without vision. Someday I'll connect with the right financier and there'll be no end to the great things I'll do.

I slow down near a newsstand and glance at the front pages to see if anybody's been killed today. The *Post* headline says, RAPIST SAYS BOOK MADE THEM DO IT. I wonder what that's all about. I pay the man, take a paper, and see a photograph of two black guys getting booked in a police station. The story is on page three. I stand at the curb, turn to the story, and read: PAPERBACK THRILLER INSPIRES RAPIST.

Two would-be rapists were foiled this afternoon by an alert pedestrian who saw them dragging a young secretary into the back of a van at the busy corner of 23rd Street and Park Avenue.

The pedestrian, Miguel Torres, tried to rescue the victim, and a brawl ensued that led to the arrival of Patrolman Dennis Wheatly and Saul Ginsberg, who arrested the alleged rapists, later identified at the 31st Precinct as Clarence Watkins and Washington Jones, both giving their residence as the Monaco Hotel on Lenox Avenue in Harlem. The van was listed as stolen.

A police spokesman said the two men made a complete confession in which they stated they got the idea for their crime from a paperback novel called "The Van Killers." The thriller was written by Mike Dunsdale and —

Holy Shit! That's one of mine! My hair stands on end and I imagine the victim's father, four uncles, eight brothers, and sixteen cousins buying guns to blow me away. The paper trembles in my hands as I read the rest of the story.

— and published by Criterion Publications of New York City. It tells the story of two young medical students who rape and murder several young women in the rear of a van.

The police spokesman said the incident proves that lewd and lascivious literature is a direct cause of crime and should be banned in New York City.

The victim's name is being withheld pending further investigation.

I run across the street to the phone booth in Nathan's and dial Criterion Publications.

McFarland comes on like the Amtrak Express. "Frapkin, where are you?"

"In a phone booth — listen, I just read the *Post* and — "

"This thing is going right through the fucking roof, Frapkin! We'll probably sell a million copies!

I clutch the phone with both hands. "Listen McFarland — whatever you do, don't give the press my name and address!"

"Why not?"

"Because some crazy son of a bitch might try and shoot me."

"Don't be ridiculous."

"I know what I'm talking about. Don't give anybody my name and address."

"But I already have."

"Good God Almighty!"

"Stop worrying so much, for chrissakes. Listen, we're arranging a nationwide publicity tour for you. When'll you be ready to leave?"

"Are you fucking crazy?"

I hang up the phone and run into the street to flag down a cab. I've got to get home fast, gather my valuables, and go into hiding before the posse gets organized. A dented cab veers toward the curb and I drive into the back seat, giving the driver my address.

As I ride downtown I can't help thinking of the horrible moral issue involved here: one of my books caused a crime to be committed. I always thought I was helping to prevent crime, because a would-be criminal, instead of beating someone to death for instance, could have the same

137

fun reading about it, and not actually have to do it, but I guess I was wrong. Guilt, guilt, guilt. And I'll probably be reincarnated as a slug next time around.

I don't have time to worry about that shit right now. I've got to calm down and try to think strategically, because my very life is in danger. It's safe to speculate that Greenberg's PR staff is calling all the papers, wire services, and TV stations to say that Mike Dunsdale is a pseudonym, and that the real author of *The Van Killers* is Alexander Frapkin who lives in Apartment 22, 123 Christopher Street. That means my pad is no longer secure but somehow I must sneak in to snatch my file of notes because if Landlord Shapiro takes the opportunity of my absence to throw all my belongings out the window, many great masterpieces will be lost to the world.

All things considered, this has to be viewed as a serious deterioration of my already badly deteriorated situation. I feel like a submarine that's just been hit by a depth charge. But I must keep pressing on, and look at the positive side. There must be a positive side someplace. I have about two grand to my name right now, and that ought to keep me going for awhile. I'll call Warmflash as soon as I can and tell him to start lawsuits on all fronts.

And if a bullet comes with my name on it, I'll try to die like a solider.

Back downtown, I approach my tenement from its rear through an alley on Bedford Street. I'm not taking the chance of going in the front door and possibly meeting reports, photographers, and citizens bent on vengeance. I sidestep past garbage cans and climb over a four-foot fence.

Ahead, fastened to the rear of my building, is a spindly fire escape. Let's hope it doesn't collapse when I'm hallway up. I look about and am surrounded by the sad backs of a dozen buildings, and above the sky is a mass of phlegm. Get moving, Frapkin — you can't afford to waste time.

I put the handle of my attaché case in my mouth, jump up, grab the bottom rung of the fire escape ladder and begin my climb. Ahead on the first floor there's a landing, and the rest of the way it's a regular staircase. When I reach the first floor I take the attaché case out of my mouth and dust myself off. I'm standing next to a window and happen to look through to see Mrs. Spagnoli mopping her bedroom floor. She spots me and nearly jumps out of her housedress, but I smile and make sign language to indicate I've locked myself out.

Up I go to the second floor, where Mr. Castelango, the drunkard, fully dressed in his longshoreman's clothes, is passed out atop a white bedspread. I hear a window opening behind me and turn around. From the tenement across the way an old guy in a T-shirt yells: "Hey, whataya doin' out dere?"

"I live upstairs and I locked myself out!"

On the third floor I see the unmade bed and the piano of a chick who's an aspiring musical comedy star and has thus far repulsed about five of my advances. Continuing my climb, on the fourth floor old Mary is standing behind her open window, a toothless grin on her face. "Your wife lock you out?"

"I locked myself out."

"But she's home — I can hear her up there."

"I guess I didn't ring loud enough."

"You two ain't gettin' along?"

"Of course we're getting along."

"Then how come she locked you out?"

"I told you I locked myself out."

Finally I reach the landing outside the window of my office, and just then something compels me to turn around. The Japanese geisha girl, completely dressed unfortunately, is looking at me, her pretty face expressionless as the Buddha's.

Turning, I knock on my window, because if Mabra's home she can admit me, and I won't have to break in as I'd originally planned.

Mabra comes running into the office screaming, "What's going on here?"

"It's me — open up!"

She peers through the grating. I wink reassuringly.

She scurries out of the office, returns with her keys, and unlocks the grating. "What is going on here?"

I crawl into my office. "Please stop screaming."

Her face is pale and distraught. "There have been telephone calls for you and people have been banging on the door. They say they are reporters and they want to talk to you about a rape. You have raped somebody?"

"Of course not."

"What are they talking about?"

"It's a long story and I don't have time to explain, but you can rest assured that I haven't raped anybody."

"You are capable of that, I think so."

I open my attaché case, lay it flat on my desk, open the

bottom drawer, pull out my folder full of precious story ideas, and lay it in the bottom of the case.

"What are you doing?"

"I'm going away for a couple of weeks."

She crosses her arms. "So you did rape somebody, and now you are running away."

"That's not true. Trust me."

"How can anyone trust you?"

I touch the tip of my finger to her cute nose. "If you don't you might find yourself back in Argentina with the synagogue burning down around you."

She slaps my finger away. I turn, open the top drawer, take out my bank book and check book, plus my stock certificates in case the Amalgamated Corporation goes up a hundred points, and drop them into my attaché case. Dashing to my dresser, I select some socks, underwear, and handkerchiefs. What else can I fit into that attaché case?

There is a knock at the door.

Mabra looks at me with the eyes of a frightened doe.

"Well go to the kitchen together," I tell her, "and you'll ask who it is."

She shakes her head. "I do not want to get involved with your rape!"

"First of all I didn't rape anybody, and secondly, if you don't help me — it's back to Argentine for you."

More knocking.

"Go ahead."

With a defeated look, she turns and heads for the front door, while I follow quietly. Approaching the door, she bends to the level of the peephole. "Who is it?" she asks, squinting.

"I'm Don Singleton of United Press. Is Alexander Frapkin home?"

"Tell him I'm not here," I whisper.

"He's not here."

"When do you expect him?"

"Tell him I've gone to California and you don't known when I'll be back."

"He has gone to California and I don't know when he'll be back."

"Do you know where he can be reached in California?"

"Tell him I'm staying at the Beverly Hills Hotel."

"He's staying at the Beverly Hills Hotel."

"May I ask who you are, ma'am?"

"Tell him you're subletting the apartment from me."

"I am subletting the apartment from you — from him — from Mr. Frapkin."

"Are you a friend of his?"

"You never met me — you got the place through a real estate agent."

"I never met him — I got the place through a real estate agent, and I wish you would leave me alone because I have got a lot of work to do."

"Thank you very much, ma'am." His footsteps shuffle down the hall.

I've got to split before one of these wise guys realizes there's a rear fire escape that a desperate character like me might use. Racing to my office, I look around excitedly, spot my thesaurus, and stuff it into my attaché case.

"When are you going to tell me what is going on?"

I grab the bottle of valiums off the bureau, twist open the

cap, and roll one out. "Why don't you take one of these?"

"I do not need drogs."

"Well I do." I toss one down my throat, cap the bottle, and throw it in the attaché case. I also throw in the Dalmanes, Dexedrine, and my plastic baggie full of Colombian buds. What else? I can't think of anything right now. I've got to travel light so I guess that'll be it. Wait a minute — the gold ring I inherited from my father — I don't want to leave it behind because it's pawnable. Taking it from its hiding place underneath my shirts, I squeeze it onto the third finger of my right hand, which suddenly becomes his hand, that crazy old father of mine. I close and latch my attaché case and head for the window.

"Where are you going?"

"If I knew, I'd tell you. If anybody comes looking for me, tell them what you just told that guy."

She holds her head in her hands. "I can't believe what has been going on since I married you. I think I am going crazy."

"Are you sure you don't want a valium?"

"I do not take drogs!"

I crawl out onto the fire escape, turn around on my hands and knees, and throw her a kiss. "Goodbye for now, my little wife. If we meet again we shall smile, and if not, then this parting is well made." I don't think she's familiar enough with English to know that's from Shakespeare.

"But what about the immigration?"

"Tell them I'm out of town on business."

With a flourish I get to my feet and commence running down the fire escape fast as I can.

Len Levinson

CHAPTER ELEVEN

I SLOW DOWN on Bedford Street two blocks from my apartment, and wonder where to go next. In Brazil a few years ago a secret underground organization of cops systematically executed people they considered undesirable, and maybe some New York cops of the same persuasion are combing the city for me right now — I wouldn't put it past them. That means I can't move into a hotel because those'll be the first places they'll look. But where am I going to hide?

I know — I'll call Jake because he's been on the lam lots of times and knows how to go about it. I'm sure he'll help me even though I insulted him a couple weeks ago.

There are bars a few blocks away on the waterfront, and I should be able to find a public telephone. I make my way through darkening streets lined with warehouses and parking lots full of trucks. Gays lurk in the shadows, hoping for love to come along. Assassination squads of police goons are spreading dragnets for me.

Ahead looms the elevated West Side Highway, closed

to traffic because it's collapsing and the city can't afford to fix it. On the other side of the highway is the Hudson River where a huge white ocean liner is docked, lit up like a mirage in the night. The air smells of salt and oil.

I turn the corner onto West Street and collide with a crowd of gays swarming outside a bar called The Roundup. They're dressed like cowboys, longshoremen, motorcycle punks, and high school kids, and probably think I'm an executive gay from uptown. I don't want to go into a gay bar so I walk uptown to the next bar, which is three blocks away, called Dodge City and also has a crowd of gays outside. I guess they've taken over the waterfront and if I want to make a phone call I'll have to go into a gay bar, but that might not be a bad idea because the assassination squads would never dream of looking for me here.

I lower the brim of my hat, throw back my shoulders, and squirm through gays to the saloon door, push it open, and walk inside. A long bar is to the left and gays are three deep in front of me; to the right is a pool table where two gays are imitating Minnesota Fats and Fast Eddie. Gays line the walls and stand around everywhere chatting, hugging, and chug-a-lugging beer out of cans. Some view me with disapproval because I left my Lone Ranger outfit home. In the far right corner a jukebox is playing rock and roll, and near it a few gays are swiveling their hips.

I walk toward a solitary gay in a Levi jacket and Abraham Lincoln beard. "There a phone in here?"

He points with his bottle of Bud. "In back."

I walk back and turn left into another large room where a bunch of gays are sitting at tables facing a stage, on which a gay with shaved head and tartar mustache is taking off his pants under a spotlight. My eyes search the room and finally come to rest on the public telephone affixed to the wall in the far corner. I walk over, drop in a dime, and dial Jake's number.

"Hello," sings the happy voice of his wife.

"Hi, Judy — this is Frapkin."

"Frapkin? Congratulations."

"What for?"

"You're famous! They were just talking about you on television."

"What did they say?"

"That two guys read one of your books and then committed a crime."

"Is the pasha there?"

"Just a minute. Jake!"

On the stage, the naked gay turns around, bends over, and shows his asshole to the audience, which applauds appreciatively. Is he going to shit bubble gum for us?

Jake picks up the phone. "How're you doin', baby?"

"Listen — I know you're probably mad at me for what I did at your party, but I'm having a problem and I need your advice."

"I'm not mad at you because I expect you to freak out from time to time. Did Judy tell you some guy from your publishing company was on television?"

"Yes."

"He said they're flooded with orders for your book. You're gonna be rich!"

"I'll have to sue to get the money, and that might take

146

years. Right now I'm afraid some law-and-order maniac might try to shoot me, and I'm looking for someplace to hide. Do you know anybody who's got a vacant cellar?"

"When you're on the lam, there's only one place to go — a whorehouse. They'll never find you in a whorehouse."

"Who do you think I am — Legs Diamond? I can't afford to live in a whorehouse."

"You could go to Australia. They can shoot you without a warrant there, but at least it's clean."

"I don't think it's necessary to go all the way to Australia."

"I can't think of anything else off hand, man, but don't live in a cellar. You're liable to turn into a mushroom."

"You've been a big help, man. I'll speak to you later."

I hang up the phone and look toward the stage. Another spotlight has come on, shining over a brutish gay man wearing jeans, a checked flannel shirt, and one golden earring. He rolls up his sleeve of his right arm, then begins applying vaseline to his hand and wrist. Surely he's not going to stick his hand up that other guy's ass. Never mind him — where are you going to stick yourself?

I close my eyes and try to think of who's got a big apartment. The only big apartments my friends could afford would be uptown on the West Side. Who do I know on the West Side? There's Danny, but he lives in a studio and he's got that big nasty Doberman. Mark deals heavy in dope so I'd better stay away from him. Marvin is a painter and you can die from the stink of turpentine. Wait a minute! My second wife Lucinda Perez, Guatemala's foremost actress in New York City — Guatemala's only

147

actress in New York City — has a big place on 160th Street and Riverdale Drive, right on the edge of Harlem. The neighborhood is as dangerous as Normandy Beach in 1944, but she's got three bedrooms and two bathrooms that're still under rent control, and she owes me a favor because I married her so she wouldn't be deported. I take my little black book, find her number, and dial.

"Hi, Lucy — this is your former husband Alexander Frapkin."

"What do you want?"

"I need a favor."

"What kind of favor?"

"I'd like you to rent me a room for a month."

"Why should I rent you a room in my apartment where I live and receive my friends?" she asks in her clipped Spanish accent.

"Because I need to drop out of sight for awhile. And let's not forget that I did you a favor when you needed it. I'm the guy who married you so you wouldn't get thrown out of this country."

"I paid you fifteen hundred dollars to marry me, so don't start pretending you're my old amigo. What have you done wrong?"

"You haven't been watching television tonight?"

"No."

"Two guys tried to rape a girl today and when the cops got them they said one of my books made them do it."

"I saw that in the paper. Is it one of yours?"

"I'm afraid so."

"Why are you afraid? The pooblicity will be good for you."

148

"I'm afraid the girl's brothers will try to shoot me, or something like that."

"Ah — I see."

"Can I hide up there for awhile?"

"Let me think."

I turn to the stage and, holy shit, it looks like the gay with the earring is actually going to stick his fist up the other gay's ass! I don't believe it — it's an anatomical impossibility, but the first gay is bent over with his hands on his knees and his ass thrust toward the audience, and the second gay is kneeling beside him and actually squeezing his fist up his ass. Astounded, I lean back against the wall and let my eyes bulge. The audience applauds appreciatively.

"Where are you?" Lucy asks.

"I'm not sure."

"I've just thought of something. It might be a good idea for you to live here for awhile because I'm trying to make my boyfriend jealous. He's been taking me for granted lately, and I have to do something."

"Does he go up there often?"

"No. that's why I want somebody here to make him jealous."

"He won't do anything to me, will he?"

"Don't be a coward."

"When can I come over?"

"I'll be home for another hour, then I'm supposed to go for an audition."

"At this time of day?"

"Already you're getting nosey."

149

"I'll be there in twenty minutes." Before she can change her mind I hang up the phone.

And on stage, the gay with the golden earring has his arm up to the elbow in the asshole of the other gay! I can't believe it, and the gays in the audience are screaming and jumping up and down, completely wigging out. The other gay turns around slowly and we can see his erection and the outline of a fist in his belly. I don't know whether to throw up, shit, pass out, or go blind, but at that very moment, the moment I'm close to total psychological disintegration, there comes swaggering up to me a short figure attired in black leather pants, black leather jacket, black leather boots, chromium chains hanging everywhere, black leather gloves stuck under an epaulette, and black leather Gestapo hat. This short figure is — heaven save me — none other than my lawyer Louis Warmflash!

"Hello, Frapkin," he says out the corner of his mouth like a tough guy. "What're you doing here?"

"I came to make a phone call."

He winks. "I had no idea you were one of us."

"I'm not." I pick up my attaché case. "Warmflash, I've got to get out of here."

"What's your hurry?"

"I've got big problems. Have you read about me in the papers today by any chance?"

"No."

"Didn't you see the story about the two guys who committed a rape because of a book they read?"

"I remember seeing the headline — you didn't write that book did you?"

150

The Last Buffoon

"I'm afraid I did, and I have reason to believe that some madman will try to kill me. I'm going into hiding right now. I'll call in a few days because I think I want to sue my publisher."

"Why don't we have a drink and discuss it right here?"

"I don't have time. See you later, Warmflash. Keep the faith."

Gripping my attaché case tightly, I weave my way around crowds of gay men who pinch me and grope me, and finally reach the street where I wave my hand in the air and try to attract a cab.

CHAPTER TWELVE

IN THE BACK SEAT of a broken-down taxicab, the full horrible significance of today hits me with full impact. I've never had so much trouble at one time in my life and I don't know if I can handle it. I'm only one fragile human being, after all. When I was younger and had problems, I used to think God was testing me. If he's still testing me he must be a sadist.

My cabdriver steers up the ramp to the section of the West Side Highway that's still operational. As we level off high in the air, I turn to the left and see a United States warship berthed beside a pier in the Hudson River. It's a beautiful ship, and I wish I were on it.

It reminds me of my earliest major defeat. When I was seventeen I tried to enlist in the Navy, intending to make it my career, but was turned down because I was underweight. If they'd taken me I'd be a happy man today, a Chief Petty Officer by this time, and in five years I'd retire with full pay for the rest of my life. Then I could write without worrying about money, and describe exotic

The Last Buffoon

ports of call, and the mystery of the sea. Instead, here I am running for my life.

I'm disgusted with my life. It keeps going from bad to worse. I don't know how much of this I can take, but I'm going to fight until the bitter end which from the looks of things isn't too far off.

The driver stops in front of the big old building where my second wife lives. I pay, drag out my attaché case, and puff steam into the chilly night as the cab accelerates away. This part of Riverdale Drive used to be a Jewish Gold Coast, but now it houses blacks and Puerto Ricans. I rush to the door and expect twenty of them to jump out of the shadows and beat me to death, for violence is the opiate of the poor. But I make it into the vestibule and press the button next to Lucy's name. The door buzzes. Entering the lobby, I see walls scrawled with obscenities. The stupid fucking peasants aren't happy unless they're defacing something, but they're driven to this by poverty just as it drives me to do terrible things too.

I take the elevator upstairs and rap on Lucy's door. She opens it. "Hello," she says, looking at me with suspicion. She's a tall, strong woman in her late twenties, and has a striking face whose characteristics suggest the grandeur of Spain, the cunning of the Indian, and the earthiness of the Negro. "Come in."

I enter her hallway, and would like to enter her enchilada.

"Let me take your hat and coat."

I give them to her.

"Have a seat."

153

I sit on the sofa and look around Lucy's living room. Her furniture is getting run down. I guess she's not doing that great either. On the walls are photographs of herself in the many roles she's played. During our marriage I saw her in a Spanish language version of *Cat on a Hot Tin Roof* and she was a real fireball.

She sits nearby on a big upholstered chair, drawing her long shapely legs underneath her and covering her knees with her skirt. Her eyes are big and brown and her hair straight and black as a horse's mane. If you saw her on the street you'd want to slow down and really check her out.

She's still examining me. "You look like hell," she says.

"I've been having a few problems."

"Can I get you something to eat?"

"Sure."

She goes to the kitchen, rattles around, and returns with a plate of rice and beans, which she places before me with a fork and napkin. I put a forkful of rice and beans in my mouth, and they're delicious, zinged with lemon juice.

"Can you listen and eat at the same time?" she asks.

I nod and continue to scoff up the chow.

"Good. Now listen carefully. For as long as you're here, I want you to answer the telephone, because I want word to get around that a man is living here. Raphael will find out sooner or later and he'll get jealous, which is what I want. Understand?"

"His name's Raphael?"

"Raphael Diaz. He's about your age but he has all his hair and he's in very good shape because he plays tennis all the time. He's a rich Cuban, and you know what they're

The Last Buffoon

like: completely out of their minds."

"Is he bigger than I am?"

"Much bigger."

"Do you think he might get violent?"

"Not if you stay calm and stick to your story that you're an old friend of mine and I'm letting you stay here for awhile. Whatever you do don't say we were married. If you get nervous and lose your temper he might become unpleasant, but you'll be too afraid to lose your temper. You need a little excitement in your life anyway. Maybe this will be something you can write about someday. Now come with me. I want to show you the apartment because I have to get gong to my audition."

She shows me the kitchen, bedrooms, linen closet, garbage chute, fire escape, and finally invites me to her boudoir, which has red drapes, a king-sized four-poster bed, an antique dresser, and a make-up table with a mirror surrounded by light bulbs. She lifts a silver container the size of a baseball from her dresser, removes the lid, and peers inside. "There are I think six hits of acid in here. If I were you I'd take two tonight, because you seem more loco in the coco than usual."

"How good is it?"

"Not very — that's why I said take two. They'll give you a nice buzz, and you know you need that. Look at yourself in the mirror."

I look and see haggard Frapkin in his undertaker suit.

She puts on her coat. "I should be back late, so don't stay up for me. Goodbye, you crazy old Jew." She slings her purse over her shoulder and heads for the door.

155

I listen to it close behind her, and her footsteps disappear into the outside hall. I'm alone at last, cleverly hidden from my enemies. All I have to worry about is a rich Cuban madman, but things could be worse. I could be falling head first out of a window.

It's very quiet in this sturdy old building. Maybe I can rent a typewriter and work in the bedroom. Maybe the Amazing Frapkin is on the comeback trail.

First I'll check the bathrooms to see if there's a razor lying around, because without this beard I'll look completely different. In Lucy's bathroom is the pink ladies' razor she shaves her legs with, and in the medicine cabinet I find an aerosol can of shaving cream and a nifty new Gillette. In the other bathroom I find another Gillette, plus a Schick, a Gem, and a Persona. I think I'll use the new Gillette, and here's a pair of scissors.

The news will be on in a few minutes, so I turn on the television set and turn it loud enough so I can hear it in the bathroom. There I undress and stare at myself in the mirror as steam from the hot leaky water faucet wafts about my head. I raise the scissors, pause, tremble, wonder whether I really should cut it off, and finally snip a swatch out of my jaw. The tuft of hair falls into my white jockey shorts, and the perfect symmetry of my face is destroyed. The deed is done.

I snip-snip-snip my left cheek and snip-snip-snip my right. Snip-snip-snip. The news comes on. The Argentine Air Force is rebelling against President Isabel Peron. Snip-snip and oh-oh-, now I remember why I grew this beard in the first place. It was to make my face look bigger and thereby make my nose look smaller — now my big honker is emerging in all its beastly glory. When I was a kid people used to say, "Is that your nose or are you playing the saxophone?" Snip-snip my mustache, snip-snip the rest of my chin, snip-snip my throat. Now I look like a sorrowful bum who needs a shave. In Lebanon the Moslems and Christians are fighting for control of the Holiday Inn.

I wash my face, smear it with lather, snap a fresh blade into the razor, position the edge near my ear, slice in, and scrape down to my chin, leaving a swathe of pink skin that hasn't seen light for eight years. The Russians are sending troops to Angola.

Scrape-scrape-scrape. I have dimples, well whataya know about that. Scrape-scrape-scrape. Look at my beautiful lips and handsome jaw. Scrape-scrape. But I've developed jowls like a walrus. Scrape-scrap. That indentation between my lower lip and chin is surely the mark of character. Scrape-scrape. The proud out-thrust of my chin is, I feel, my best feature. Scrape-scrape. I'm almost finished now, and you know, I don't look bad at all except for that pouch in front of my throat and my big nose. Irish terrorists are holding a London couple hostage in their flat.

I rinse my face, put on more lather, and shave against the grain for that smooth satin finish. I think I look younger without a beard — if only I had more hair on my head I might pass for thirty-five and be able to hustle young girls who like men with big noses. How strange to touch the skin of my face after all these years.

I rinse again, dry off, study my face, use another mirror

so I can see more angles, and decide that I really don't look that Jewish. I could be a Spanish grandee, an Italian diplomat, a Turkish poet. Maybe I should give myself a phony Italian name for additional camouflage. I could easily pass for an Italian, and I know all about Italian food, Catholicism, and the Mafia. But what Italian name? Hold on! My nose has a certain resemblance to Jimmy Durante's. Rink-a-dink-a-doo. I'll call myself Joe Durante and pretend to be Jimmy's third cousin on his father's side. Everybody loved Jimmy Durante and will be so overcome by sentimental memories that they'll never think of accusing me of being Jewish. When the big pogrom comes I'll be safe, but who's that strange guy looking at me in the mirror. What an interesting face he has. I'll be he could get laid if he really wanted to. They're rioting in Timor.

My misfortunes have been a blessing in disguise — I've rediscovered my face. The Subtleties of its features, blurred over for so long, is influencing the texture of my mind, making it more subtle. I can actually feel this happening, or at least I think I can. Now I'll take a shower to wash all this hair off me, and maybe then I'll drop some acid.

Two paperback rapists were arraigned in Criminal Court today.

I run to the living room and see reporters holding microphones near the mouth of a black man.

"Naw," he says, "we wasn't gonna kill her. We was just gonna have some fun."

The handsome announcer comes on and says the district attorney is under pressure from various women's groups to ask for life imprisonment with no possibility of

The Last Buffoon

parole. He adds that the author of *The Van Killers*, Alexander Frapkin, still has not been available for comment. Then a Brooklyn councilman comes on and makes an emotional statement in favor of the censorship of literature detrimental to society. Finally Joe Greenberg is interviewed in his office, seated behind his desk. His tie is in place and his suit jacket on.

"Lissen here," he tells the reporter, "are you trying to say that those two guys never would've tried to rape somebody if they hadn't read this book?" The smart bastard holds up a copy and the camera obligingly zooms in. "Both of those guys've got records for burglary, robbery, felonious assault, breaking and entering, narcotics — they're not exactly choirboys. A book," he wags it before the cameras, "doesn't make anybody do anything they wouldn't do anyway. Censorship is a phony issue here."

"Can you tell us anything about Alexander Frapkin, the author of *The Van Killers*?"

"He's a good writer, like all the writers we publish."

"Why do you suppose he's been unavailable for comment?"

"When you find him, tell me. By the way, he's written seven other books for us, and as far as I know, nobody's committed any crimes because of them."

The camera zooms in on my masterpieces arrayed on his desk. What fantastic publicity it is! I must call Warmflash in the morning and tell him to sue for my royalties. Even after he takes his cut I should have enough left to keep going for a few years in a cheap sunny place where I can write a popular best-seller that'll make me rich

159

forever.

A commercial for denture powder comes on. I turn off the TV and return to the bathroom. A strange swarthy fellow looks at me from the mirror, and if his nose were filled with nickels he'd be a millionaire. I take a piss, look in the mirror some more, and notice that my smooth face doesn't coordinate well with my longish unruly hair, or what's left of it. A haircut is in order.

I find some hand mirrors in Lucy's bedroom, position them around the bathroom so I can see all parts of my dome, and start cutting. Snip-snip-snip. Won't my friends be surprised when they see me.

I cut until it's about an inch long all around, then part and comb it. Next I brush the shorn clumps from my shoulders, clean the floor, put away the mirrors, and take a long shower. Emerging from the tub like a wet sea god, I dry off, don clean underwear and a silk man's robe I find in a closet, and wonder what to do next.

Rrriiiiinnnnnggggg.

Where the hell's her telephone?

Rrriiiiinnnnnggggg.

There's one beside the living room chair. "Hello?"

Silence on the other end.

"Hello?" I say again.

Nothing. I hang up the phone.

I'm not sleepy. What should I do? I think I'll drop the acid.

In Lucy's bedroom I open the silver pot. The acid is inside, yellow stains on little squares of paper. I lift two out. Should I do it? I go through this every time, staring at the

acid fearfully, hopefully, indecisively. Oh what the hell —
it can't kill me. Even if it's a bad trip it'll be over in twelve
hours, but the odds are against a bad trip, and a good trip
would be so helpful right now.

I carry two hits to the kitchen, pour myself a glass of
water, and stop cold again. Should I do it? Oh, for
chrissakes, stop being such a scaredy-cat. I open my mouth,
put the paper in, and wash it down with the water.

The deed is done. There's no turning back now. Gulp.

I break out in a cold sweat. What if the Nazis come for
me again? I can feel it — it's going to be another
concentration camp trip — another horror show — but
wait a minute! I've got a bottle of valiums and if the trip
gets too bad I can always take a few and come down. To
make sure, I run to my room, claw through my attaché
case, and find them, plus the Dalmanes. I relax — these'll
be my life preservers. I put them in the pocket of this robe
where they'll be close at all times.

Okay, what should I do until the acid hits. I'm too
nervous to look at magazines, and TV might be a downer,
so I think I'll sit on the floor and do Buddhist meditation. I
lay a sofa cushion on the floor, sit cross-legged on it, rest
my hands in my lap, and close my eyes.

Fifteen minutes have passed. When's this goddamn
stuff going to hit? I don't feel anything and I'm getting
uptight just waiting. Maybe I should take one more hit. I
go to Lucy's bedroom, get another one, carry it to the
kitchen, and wash it down with orange juice.

Rrrriiinnnngggg.

"Hello?"

161

Silence, then a click. Somebody's playing fuck-around with Lucy's phone.

I sit on the floor again. I don't think CRACK this acid is any good WHACK anymore. Maybe it's been around BZZZZZZZ too long and lost it's power. What a dragggggggGGGGGGGGGGGGGGGGGGGGGGGGGGGOOO OOOOOOOOOOOOOOOOOOOHHHHHHHHHHHH HHHHHHHHHHHZZZZZZZZZZZZZZZZZZXXXXX XXXXXXXXXXXXXXXXKKKKKKKKKKKKKKKKKKK KRRRRRRRRRRRRRRRRRRRRQQQQQQQQQQQ QQQQQQQQQBBBBBBBBBBBBBBBBBBBBUUUU UUUUUUUUUUUUUUUZZZZZZZZZZZZZZ ZZZZZOOOOOOOOOOOOOOOOOOOOOLLLLLL LLLLLLLLLLLLLVVVVVVVVVVVVVVVVVVVB ONGBONGBONGOBANGBANGBANGOBBBBBBZ *ZZZZZZZZZZZZZZZZZZZ*AAAAAAAAAAAAAAAAA AAPPPPPPPPPPPPPPPPPPPPWWWWWWWWWWH HHHHHHHHHHHHHHHHHHHHAAAAAAAAAAAA AAAAAAAAAPPPPPPPPPPPPPPPPPPPPP

BRIGHTNESS!

I open my eyes and see a Latin man pointing a gun at my nose!

"*Quién es?*" he asks, a menacing tone in his voice. He's wearing a double-breasted suit and a thin mustache, and he must be Lucy's crazy Cuban boyfriend.

"I'm sorry, but I don't speak Spanish," I reply, terrified and tripping and lying in the middle of the living room rug.

"Who are you?" he asks in a heavy Spanish accent.

162

"Alexander Frapkin."

"What are you doing een here?"

"I just got evicted, and Lucy said I could stay here for awhile. She and I are old friends, you see."

"You and Lucinda are old friends how?"

"I used to date a friend of hers."

"Which friend?"

"I don't remember."

"I theenk you're lying. When's Lucinda coming home?"

"How should I know?"

He taps the gun barrel against the bridge of my nose. "Do not get smart weeth me, greengo." His eyeballs are popping and in the middle of his forehead is a vein like the Alaska pipeline.

"Please don't shoot me," I plead, shaking from head to foot. "I have a daughter."

"Why don't you stay weeth her?"

"She's only four years old and she lives with her mother who hates me."

He raises his left nostril. "I theenk you are having a love affair weeth Lucinda,"

"Don't be ridiculous. She'd never have an affair with somebody like me."

He looks me over. "That ees true." He checks out his watch. "I weel wait until she comes home, and then we weel see where she has been. Go to bed."

"Yes sir."

I go to the bedroom, shut the door, crawl under the

covers, and close my eyes. The sheets smell like perfume. Maybe Lucy's sexy sister slept here last. With a happy smile I drift away.

• • •

Screaming!

I sit up in bed. Sunlight aureoles behind the drawn curtain; my watch says ten o'clock. The yelling is outside my door. I tiptoe over, open up a crack, and see Lucinda and the mad Cuban squared off in the living room.

"*Puta!*" he yells.

"*Maricón!*" she shrieks.

She throws an ashtray at him and scores a direct hit on the shoulder he tries to hide behind. He throws his gun at her but she ducks out of the way. She hits him over the head with a lamp. He punches her in the mouth. She scratches his face. He grabs her arm. She tries to kick him in the balls. He wraps his arms around her waist and kisses her. She sighs and runs her fingers through his hair. He picks her up and carries her to the bedroom. The door closes behind them.

I must get dressed and start making important phone calls.

164

CHAPTER THIRTEEN

"**HELLO, MR. FRAPKIN.** Mr. Warmflash has been trying to reach you. Hang on a second."

Clack.

"Where are you, Frapkin?"

"I'm staying with a friend of mine."

"You'd better call your wife fast!"

"What's the problem?"

"She claims that you and I swindled her out of a few thousand dollars, and she's threatening to go to the police."

"A few thousand dollars? How come I only got one thousand out of it?"

"Don't you think I'm entitled to make a living?"

"You've got a bite like a fucking crocodile, Warmflash."

"I want you to call Mabra right away."

"Where the hell is she?"

"You can reach her through her doctor, Sidney Siegel. His number is — "

"I know what his number is — he's fucking my wife.

165

Listen, about my royalties, I want you to initiate lawsuits without delay."

"I can't initiate anything unless I have your contracts."

"I'll send them to you in a few days. How long is this going to take?"

"From three to six years."

"What!"

"You heard me."

"How much money do you think we'll get?"

"That depends on how well your books sell."

"They'll sell fantastically with all this publicity, and we'll split everything fifty-fifty, right?"

"Wrong, because you'll have to pay court fees, my expenses, taxes, and so forth. Your share will probably amount to around forty percent."

"That's all?"

"What did you expect — an oil well?"

"I think I should've been a lawyer."

"You're too indecisive to be a lawyer."

"What makes you say that?"

"I've been dealing with you for years, and you never know whether you're coming or going."

"I know whether I'm coming or going."

"What you need is a good stiff cock up your ass, and I'm just the man to give it to you."

"Warmflash, I can't believe you just said that."

"Why don't you come over to my place tonight? We can have a little wrestling match."

"Oh God."

"I have a movie projector and we can watch a new film

The Last Buffoon

I've bought called *San Francisco Rough Trade*."

I hang up the phone and scratch my head. Then I go to the kitchen, pour myself a glass of orange juice, and carry it to the telephone, where I call my wife's boyfriend.

"Hiya, Sid."

"Who's this?"

"Frapkin."

"Where the hell have you been?"

"None of your fucking business. I just spoke to Warmflash and he told me your girlfriend misses me so much she's going crazy. Is she there?"

"She's working."

"Tell her I'll be home in a few weeks, and that I haven't forgotten her or our arrangement."

"You're not trying to pull a fast one, are you?"

"The only fast one I pull is between my legs."

I hang up the phone, go to the kitchen, and fry three eggs for breakfast. While eating them something is nagging in the back of my mind, and that something is Joe Greenberg. I'll bet that sonofabitch lives like a prince, while I'm living out of my attaché case. He owes me a fortune and it galls me that I can't get it. After breakfast I'm going to call him and run a number over his head. I'll have to use an outside phone so he can't trace me here.

When the last morsel is gone from my plate, I throw it and the frying pan into the sink, put on my hat and coat, and leave the apartment.

Outside the sky is oily and the sun completely obliterated. Five young Puerto Ricans shuck and jive toward me and maybe they'll cut my throat and end my

167

worries. They walk by and I arrive safely at the corner of 160th Street and Broadway.

I'm the only Caucasian in sight, a foreigner in my own country. Lining Broadway are bodegas, cuchi-frito parlors, a Cuban-Chinese restaurant, a fruit and vegetable stand that sells things I've never imagined could grow, and a candy and cigarette store, some bars, and a pizza stand right on the corner. I think I'll go there and see if they have a phone.

It's warm and pungent inside, and on stools sit Puerto Rican teenagers of the sort who carve out people's hearts for laughs. The Puerto Rican guy behind the counter has a mustache, tomato-stained apron, and questioning look.

I stick my finger in the air and pretend to dial. "*Teléfono?*"

"It's over there," he says in peppery English, pointing toward the back of the shop.

I get in the phone booth, pull the door shut, and see phone numbers and obscenities scratched everywhere. One wag has written EAT SHIT AND SAVE ON THE HIGH COST OF FOOD. A great inflation slogan if I ever saw one. The President ought to mention it in his next televised speech on the economy. I drop a dime in the slow and dial.

"Mr. Greenberg's office."

"This is Alexander Frapkin and I want to speak to him."

"Please hold on."

Zzzzzaaaaaaaaapppppppp.

"Hello, Alex — so good to hear from you," Joe Greenberg purrs.

168

"I want my money."

"What money?"

"The money you owe me."

"Are you going on the publicity tour?"

"Never."

"Then you're not getting any money."

"Okay — listen to this, you scumbag," I say threateningly. "I'm not asking for charity. You owe me money and I want it. If I don't receive a large check from you within seven days, I will not see a lawyer, I will not go to court — I'll take care of you myself, and if you wonder what I mean, just use your imagination a little."

"Are you threatening me?"

"If you don't pay me everything you owe me, I'm going to kill you," I tell him.

"Frapkin, you've got in over your head this time. I'm calling the police right now."

"I don't care if you call the mayor or the CIA. Someday you'll be walking along and I'll come out of nowhere and blow your fucking brains out!"

Click.

How terrible that an honest citizen like me has to do things like this to get paid.

While I'm in the phone booth I think I'd better call one of my contacts and try to get a book assignment. I need to pile up a cash reserve so I can relax and take my time while writing my big one. The sooner I get money the sooner I can get started. I find the appropriate number in my little black book, drop a dime in the slot, and dial.

"Brunswick Publishing."

Len Levinson

"Selma Sapperstein, please."

Crack bong.

"Hello?" she says, a middle-aged bleached blonde with several screws missing.

"Hello Selma, this is Alexander Frapkin."

"To what do I owe this pleasure?"

"Financial insolvency. You got a book you want written?"

"I thought you were making a bundle at Criterion."

"I am, but they won't give it to me. Have you got something?"

"How about a porno?"

"No porno. I jerk off too much."

"Mafia?"

"I just wrote one and I want a change."

"A cop?"

"Who is he?"

"Joe Benson, your standard New York detective who hates everybody and doesn't want to know from the Miranda decision. Interested?"

"How much?"

"What do you care? We're not going to pay you either."

"That's not funny, Selma."

"The usual fifteen hundred dollars. You'll get half within thirty days after you turn in the manuscript, and then rest within the next thirty days."

"That sounds like a crock of shit."

"It is."

"What else do I have to know about this Benson?"

"He's a big ugly guy and he's got black hair. His wife

170

runs around on him. Yours will be number four in a series. How soon can you get it to us?"

"A few days."

"Don't forget — lots of blood and lots of rough sex."

"I won't forget. Speak to you soon, Selma."

I hang up, and it looks like I'm still in the ballgame. I'll do a Benson and immediately thereafter a Mafia, and that ought to make me financially secure for long enough to write my long-awaited popular best-seller.

• • •

It's three o'clock in the morning. Stealthily I carry my attaché case and shopping bag full of groceries up the stairs of my building on Christopher Street. My plan is to hide out in my own apartment where no one would think of looking for me, and work in peace.

A door opens and I hear footsteps coming down the stairs. Secret Agent Frapkin freezes. The footsteps come closer — a cowboy homosexual, a motorcycle homosexual, and a longshoreman homosexual. The cowboy lives on the top floor and does a lot of cruising. We've said hello a few times but I don't think he knows my story as well as I know his. I crouch behind my shopping bag and climb two more flights to my door. Silently I insert the keys and turn the locks. I push the door open, reach around, and click on the kitchen light. My refrigerator, stove, and protein chart taped to the wall haven't gone anywhere. Home sweet home.

It smells like soap commingled with Mabra's perfume, but the sofa's empty. She must be in the arms of Dr. Sidney Siegel right now, while I must gather my resources to write yet another book.

The Dexedrine I took to get me home still is coursing through my veins, and I don't feel like going to bed. Perhaps a homecoming celebration is in order. I think I'll smoke a joint and listen to Wagner.

I put away the food, change into jeans, and light up. Flipping the switches on my stereo, the dial glows mint green. It's an expensive set purchased when I was in the big time, and I hope no junkie rips it off because I could never replace it. I plug in the headphones so my neighbors won't be bothered, clamp the cups over my ears, position the record, light a stick of sandalwood incense, and lie on the sofa.

The first eerie strains of "The Flight of the Valkyries" pierces the silence, and I look out the window at the night sky. In the smoggy darkness over the rooftops a quarter of the moon hangs like a crooked smile. A thousand Valkyries fly past, their white gowns iridescent in the moonlight. They're carrying the souls of dead warrior-artists to Valhalla, and someday they'll take me along, but right now I'm at the beginning of a great new cop book for which I probably never will get paid.

CHAPTER FOURTEEN

BENSON GRABBED THE KID and threw him against the wall. "Okay, you little bastard, what you got on you!"

"I wanna see my lawyer!" Benson raised his .44 and hit the kid in the face, the cold steel mashing lips and teeth. "I said what you got on you!"

The kid tried to speak, but blood burbled out his mouth. Benson slapped him down and found three glassine envelopes of junk tucked into his sock. "Where'd you get these?"

The kid shook his head. Benson whacked him with the .44 again, opening a ragged gash on his cheek. "You'd better start talking, fucker, or you're dead."

"I don't know nothin'!"

Benson punched the barrel of the .44 into the kid's mouth, knocking teeth and gums back to his throat. Benson's finger tightened around the trigger, and perspiration dripped from the kid's forehead.

"I'm gonna count to three," Benson cried, "and if you don't start talking by then, you can say goodbye to your head."

173

Len Levinson

The kid trembled; his eyes begged for mercy.
"One."

Somebody is inserting a key in the front door. I jump from my desk and hide behind the dresser, looking to see if it'll be the extermination squad, a report, or Shapiro the landlord here to throw all my belongings out the window.

The door opens, Mabra walks in, stares at my face. "You have shaved off your beard!"

"How do you like the new me?"

"You look very different."

"Do you think I look better or worse?"

"I don't know — turn sideways please."

I give her my left and right profile. "Well?"

She shrugs. "Not better and not worse. Why didn't you tell me you were home?"

"I've been busy."

"You and I have to go for an interview at the Immigration on the 10th of December.

"What for?"

"Mr. Warmflash says they are become very suspicious of marriages like ours. He says we will have to make up a good story of how we met and everything. Since you are a writer, maybe you can do it?"

"I'm working on a new book and I don't have time. What're you doing here this time of day — quit your job?"

"This is my day off."

"I'm surprised you're spending it here. I'd think Dr. Sidney Siegel's apartment would be more comfortable."

"I have told you many times that he and I are none of your business."

174

The Last Buffoon

"I've got to get back to work. Try to be quiet, okay?"

"Okay."

I return to my office and close the door.

"But he'll kill me if I tell you!"

"I'll kill you if you don't. Two!"

"Okay, okay." The kid's face was streaked with blood, sweat, and tears.

"Start talking."

"You gotta protect me!"

"Where'd you get that junk?"

"From the Man."

"What man?"

"I don't know his name."

"What's he look like?"

"A big black dude."

Benson holstered his .44 and grabbed the kid by the scruff of his neck. "Let's go."

Benson dragged the kid out of the alley, the kid's sunglasses shattered and askew on his nose.

I'm in Bazoomingdales, approaching the sunglass counter. I'm wearing my freshly cleaned and mended Burberry trenchcoat, Borsalino hat, and matching accessories. Swirling around are hundreds of beautiful rich broads.

Approaching is a young salesgirl who looks like she just stepped out of the pages of *Vogue*. "May I help you?"

"I'm interested in purchasing a pair of sunglasses, preferably French-made in the popular aviator design."

"Gold or silver?"

"Silver."

"Surely."

She walks past a thousand blank eyes and bends over, displaying the kind of ass you'd like to bite. She takes out a display board, which she carries to me. "Try this pair on," she says, holding out shades.

I hook them on and look in the mirror. "May I try on the others?"

"Surely."

An important choice must be made, and the *Vogue* model is impatient to hear it, but I dare not act precipitously, for my future well-being hands in the balance here. I try them all on, and then do it again. I narrow them down to two, and am stymied. "Which of these do you think I look best in?"

"That one." She points to a pair that makes me look professional.

I put on the other pair, which makes me look like a movie star. "I think these are a little better."

"No, in my opinion the others are more attractive on you."

I put them on and look at myself from all the angles. Maybe she's right.

"Yes," she says, her earrings dangling, "those are much better."

"How much are they?"

"Twenty-five thirty-nine." I reach into my pocket for the cabbage.

"You're certain I look best in these?"

She smiles. "They make you look distinguished."

I hand her the money. "What're you doing after work tonight?"

"Why do you ask?"

"I thought perhaps we could get together for a drink."

"I'm afraid not."

"Why?"

"You're old enough to be my father."

"They say old wine is best."

"Then I'll have something to look forward to when I'm old, won't I?" she walks away with the money, rings it up, and brings me change. "Shall I put them in a bag?"

"I'll wear them. You know, they say that May and September make a delightful combination."

"I've heard September say that, but, curiously, never May."

"Little girl, you're awfully sharp."

"Mister, I know it." She walks off to wait on an old biddy.

Moving from the counter, I can't help thinking that if I were rich and famous like Norman Mailer, she'd meet me afterwards for a glass of wine, and maybe around midnight she'd let me eat her. Once again my lack of success is hindering my love life. I'd better return home immediately and go to bed early, so I can arise early tomorrow and resume work on Benson. As soon as I get the advance I'll write an important significant novel, and then after it's reviewed in the *Time* and sold to the movies, I'll come back here and sweep the little bitch off her feet.

177

Len Levinson

CHAPTER FIFTEEN

BENSON PUSHED OPEN THE DOOR and walked inside the saloon. Some people were sitting at tables and some sat at the bar. They all looked at him with suspicion. He tightened his grip on the .44 and walked to the man in the cashmere coat, halfway down the bar.

"I want to talk to you," Benson said to him.

The man turned around, his highball glass in hand. He had sleepy eyes and a droopy mustache. "Who're you?"

Benson showed his shield. "Detective Joe Benson, 21st Precinct."

"Whataya want?"

"You."

The man laughed. "Come back later — I'm busy right now."

Benson pulled out his .44 and pointed it between the man's eyes. "Let's go, fucker."

The man made a motion toward his pocket, but Benson hit him hard with

178

The Last Buffoon

Someone is knocking at my door. I sit still and wait for them to give up and go away. More knocking. Then I hear a key turning the lock. The Puerto Rican super enters my kitchen, followed by two guys in topcoats and fedoras. I walk toward them. "What's going on?"

The front guy pulls a badge out of his pocket. "Police."

He looks just like Benson, and I'm wondering if I've fallen into my novel, like Alice through the looking glass. I've got to stop smoking so much dope.

Johnny the super shrugs his skinny shoulders as if to say he doesn't know what's going on.

"I'm Detective Jenkins," says the front cop, "and this is Detective Burke. Are you Alexander Frapkin?"

"I am."

"We'd like to talk with you."

My mind is malfunctioning at the speed of light. First of all, I don't think this is a hallucination. Second, if it's a drug bust they would've shown me a search warrant by now. "Why don't you come in the living room and sit down?"

"I gotta go," Johnny says.

"Thanks for helpin' us out," says Burke.

Johnny leaves me and I'm without a witness, but I think I can handle it. I lead the cops into the living room. "Can I take your coats?"

"We won't be here that long."

"Have a seat."

They fall onto my sofa and look around at my stereo, TV set, and poster reproduction of Avalokitesvara, the Buddha of Ultimate Compassion, who's useless as usual. I sit on the leather chair and wonder what the fuck is going on.

Jenkins takes out a notepad. "We're here on a complaint that you threatened to kill a Joe Greenberg. What can you tell us about that?"

"I never threatened to kill him. He's lying."

"Did you have a telephone conversation with Joe Greenberg on the morning of November 28th?"

"I believe I might have."

"Do you remember what you talked about?"

"He owes me some money, and I supposed I asked for it."

"And you didn't threaten to kill him?"

"Oh no, sir. I told him I'd turn the matter over to my lawyer."

"What's your lawyer's name?"

"Louis Warmflash. His office is at 315 West 42nd Street."

"Do you own a gun, Mr. Frapkin?"

"No."

Jenkins looks at Burke. They stand up.

"Mr. Frapkin, if anything happens to Mr. Greenberg, we'll be back."

They were such nice guys, so respectful of my civil rights, so reasonable. How can I portray them as fascist pigs in my books? Well, they've got the Policeman's Benevolent Association to look after them, and all I've got is my gay lawyer, whom I'd better call without delay.

"What is it now, Frapkin?"

"My publisher told the cops I threatened his life, which

of course is true. The cops are on their way to see you right now, so tell them what a nice gentle guy I am."

"My, what an exciting life you lead, Frapkin. You never know about some people. Mabra told me you're back home. I can reach you there?"

"Yes."

"How about inviting me over for a frankfurter sometime?"

"Warmflash, you're a distinguished citizen and a member of the bar. Will you please stop trying to fuck me?"

"I've always been attracted to shady characters."

"How can you call anybody a shady character, you leather queen?"

"Let's you and me play drop-the-soapy in the shower sometime, Frapkin."

"Let's try to bring our relationship back to the squalid professional level where it was before I found out you're a fag, okay? Now having settled that, can you tell me how my lawsuits are proceeding against Criterion Publications?"

"We've filed our papers and we're waiting for a court date, but I wouldn't raise my hopes too high if I were you. All the publicity has died out, and that means your books probably are selling the way they always sell, which is to say poorly. You know how it is, Frapkin. One day you're on the bottom, and next day you're still on the bottom. The public is fickle. They have a short memory. But I have a long cock that I'd like to place ever so gently between your buns.

"I'm hanging up right now, Warmflash. You're my

lawyer and I'm your client, but good day."

I sit at my desk, my spine collapsing. I thought I was going to make some big money out of this lawsuit, but it doesn't look that way. Shit. Fuck. Piss. Yet I can't let this setback stop me. I must fight on, secure in the belief that in the end I shall emerge triumphant.

• • •

I storm into the grungy office of the Housing Authority on lower Broadway. I'm wearing torn jeans and a moth-eaten topcoat saved for situations like this. "Who's in charge here?" I scream.

The center of the room is crammed with a hundred grumbling people sitting on chairs, and around the cubicles where complaints are taken.

A harried social worker broad comes up to me. "May I help you?"

"I want to speak to the person in charge here."

"You have a complaint against your apartment?"

"That's right."

"I'm afraid you'll have to sit and wait your turn."

"If I sit over there I'm liable to infect those people, because I've got a hundred and one fever. You see, there's a broken window in my apartment and the landlord won't fix it." Cough, cough, cough.

I pound my chest and follow her across the room to her cubicle, where we sit down. She has blue eyes, a mole on her chin, and her light hair is combed into a bun. "Your name please?"

"Alexander Frapkin."

"Your address?"

The Last Buffoon

I take out my wallet and hand her my driver's license.

She writes on her form. "You said you have a broken window?"

"In my bathroom. I called the landlord months ago, but he won't fix it."

"Who's your landlord?"

"Murray Shapiro — you've probably heard of him. He's the worst slumlord in New York. Why don't you people put him behind bars?"

"Have you seen a doctor?"

"I can't afford a doctor."

"What're you taking for your fever?"

"Anything I can get my hands on. Have you got a pill that perhaps you could recommend?"

She shuffles some papers. "We'll notify Mr. Shapiro of this violation, and if he doesn't fix it within thirty days, we'll fix it ourselves and send him the bill."

"Why don't you send an inspector over? He'd find a hundred violations and then you could issue Shapiro a subpoena."

"I ought to issue *you* a subpoena." She throws the form on a pile. "Next!"

The door was opened by a glamorous blonde in a negligee. Her eyes were blue and her breasts substantial. There was a mole in her chin.

He showed his badge. "I'm Detective Benson from the 21st Precinct. Are you Miss Shapiro?"

"Yes."

"I heard you have some information for me."

183

"Please come in."

He entered her large luxurious living room, and she locked the door behind them. "Would you like a drink?"

"I don't drink on duty."

"Do you sit down on duty?"

He walked across the room and sat on the sofa. "What's the information?"

She sat opposite him on a chair, and when she crossed her legs he could see she wasn't wearing underwear. She wasn't a real blonde either. "Actually I wanted to talk about Clarence Watkins, who you arrested last night in Harlem. I wonder if you'd consider dropping your charges against him."

"What's he to you?"

She looked him squarely in the eye. "He's my boyfriend."

"You'd better find another boyfriend, because he's going away for a long time."

She stood up, pulled a piece of lace, and her negligee fell away. She was naked as hell and beautiful as heaven.

Hey that's a real nice line, Frapkin. And you didn't even plagiarize it from anybody.

"Are you sure there isn't anything I can do to change your mind?"

He reached down and unzipped his fly. "I don't know. What can you do?"

She walked toward him tantalizingly, dropped to her knees, and reached for his

Rrriiinnnnnnnnngggggggg.

184

"Hello."

"Frapkin?"

"Speaking."

"This is Selma Sapperstein at Brunswick. We're spinning a new cop series off Benson, so change his name to Mike Shanahan and keep going."

"But I've already got it half-finished!"

"So you'll only have to make half the corrections."

"What'll I do about Benson's wife?"

"Push her off a cliff. Shanahan isn't married."

"Do you realize how much extra work you're making for me?"

"If you don't want to write the book, don't. I've got a hundred starving writers out there who will."

"I'll do it."

"Of course you'll do it. I'll see you when it's finished, Frapkin. Goodbye."

I hang up the phone and grit my teeth. I don't know how much more of this shit I can take. The muses put obstacles in our paths to stiffen our muscles for the steep upward climb toward success, or at least that's what Segovia said, and I'll try to keep it in mind as I go back and make all the fucking changes. Where is my Maxwell Perkins?

CHAPTER SIXTEEN

I'M SITTING WITH MABRA and a dozen other married couples, some with lawyers, in a waiting room at the Bureau of Immigration, waiting to be interviewed. In hushed tones the lawyers rehearse their clients to make sure their phony stories jibe, but Warmflash chose not to come because he was here with me before and doesn't want to arouse the suspicion that he and I have a racket going. Mabra and I go over our story for the last time. I had to dream it up because she has no imagination.

We're called into the cubicle of an official named Ms. Riley, who wears her gray hair at earlobe length and is a fussy old maid. She looks us over, and I must say we're a handsome couple today, me in my basic blue suit, and Mabra in jewels and a wool skirt fastened with a gold safety pin. Ms. Riley asks some general questions about my application, and then requests that Mabra leave so the cross-examination of me can begin. When she's finished with me she'll question Mabra alone, and then compare stories. If they don't match up, Mabra will return to

Argentina, and I'll be prosecuted.

The cubicle is battleship gray and in a row with other cubicles where officials are popping questions. Ms. Riley looks up from the papers on her desk and smiles like a weasel about to grab a hare. "It says here you've been married before, Mr. Frapkin." Her false teeth gleam in florescent lighting, and I realize that was a question.

"I've been married twice before, Ms. Riley."

"You're second wife was also an alien?"

"Yes she was from Guatemala."

Ms. Riley's eyes light up like a pinball machine. "You've married two aliens?"

"I'm attracted to exotic women, I guess.

"How long did your marriage to the Guatemalan last?"

"About six months."

"That's all?"

"Her career made severe demands on our marriage. She was an actress, and actors and actresses get married and divorced all the time."

"But only six months — my, my."

"Mabra and I won't have that problem. She's not an actress."

"What does she do?"

"She's a nurses' helper at New York University Hospital."

"How did you meet her?"

I look at the ceiling as if trying to remember the details. "We met last January 20th in Central Park. I recall that it was a beautiful day — the sky was clear and the sun shone brightly on newly fallen snow. I was ice skating in the

Wollman Rink — it's one of my favorite pastimes — when suddenly a girl fell down in front of me. I stopped and took her arm in an effort to help her up, and when she looked at me, I realized I was gazing into the eyes of the most beautiful girl I'd ever seen in my life. That's how I met my wife."

Ms. Riley's eyes have that faraway look. "What did you say to her, Mr. Frapkin?"

"It was something like: 'I think I've found you at last.'"

"And what did she say?"

"She said: 'You're the first person who's ever said that to me.'"

"And what did you say then?"

"I invited her to have a cup of coffee with me in the pavilion."

Ms. Riley moves to the edge of the chair. "And then what happened?"

"I want this Shanahan dead," said Duke Blackstone.

"He's tough," replied Needles. "It won't be easy."

"Nobody's tougher than a bullet. Take as many of the boys as you need and gun the motherfucker down."

"The boys are afraid of him. He damn near beat Clarence Wilkins to death in the Bahama Bar, and he shot how many others? Six?"

Blackstone slammed his fist on his huge mahogany desk so hard the papers on it fluttered. "What is it with you fuckin' bums? You're afraid of one stupid cop? If I wasn't so busy I'd take him off myself." He pointed his Egyptian cigarette at Needles. "Get going, and don't come back unless it's to tell me

188

that the pig is dead."
  Needles stood up and put on his big hat. "Okay, boss."

I lean back in the chair and look at my watch. It's twenty minutes after midnight, and my brain is turning into oatmeal. I've been working on this fucking book day and night for eight days in a row. I can't go on like this. If I don't take some time off soon I'll have a total physical and mental breakdown.

Tomorrow I think I'll get high and go to a movie, maybe splurge afterwards and have dinner in one of those macrobiotic restaurants in the East Village. I won't think of Shanahan at all. Fuck Shanahan.

I roll a Dalmane out of the bottle I keep on my dresser, because I want to get knocked out fast. It'll make me stupid tomorrow, but I'm taking the day off and it won't matter.

Like Frankenstein I make my way to the sink for water. The sofa is empty — Mabra hasn't been here for two weeks. We're just about finished, but that's the way it goes. She'll marry Dr. Sidney Siegel and someday I'll be found slumped over my typewriter. The great Nijinsky once said that all writers are martyrs, and in my case that's certainly the truth.

CHAPTER SEVENTEEN

SHANAHAN GOT OUT of the Plymouth. Stretching, he was about to slam the door when he heard a soft metallic snick. He dropped to the ground just as a gun exploded, and a bullet crashed into the wall behind him. He lay still. There was silence for a few seconds.

"I got him!" somebody shouted.

"You sure?"

"I toldja I never miss."

There was a rustle of feet, and Shanahan opened one eye. From behind the cars in front of him he saw

The front door is opening. I look and see Mabra entering the kitchen. I go out to greet her.

"My notification came from the Immigration today," she says. "Mr. Warmflash said I can move away now."

My jeweled maiden is leaving me. I drop into the leather chair.

"I have been taking my things away little by little," she says. "There are only a few things left." She brings a suitcase form the closet and fills it with frilly things.

"Are you moving in with Dr. Sidney Siegel?"

"I am getting an apartment of my own. I have a new job, you know."

"Doing what?"

"Executive assistant to a vice president of the Schaumberger Corporation."

"What do they do?"

"They import shoes from all over the world. I will be in charge of Latin America."

"You're really moving up in the world."

"I am not a dreamer like you."

She goes to the bedroom and finished packing, while I watch mournfully.

"I guess that's all," she says, folding a skirt into the suitcase.

"Would you like me to carry your suitcase downstairs?"

"Thank you very much, but I can manage myself." She lifts it and walks to the door. "Mr. Warmflash will send you the check for the rest of the money I owe you."

"When will that be?"

"In about two weeks, right after I get my green card." She drops her set of keys on the table and unlatches the door. "Well, goodbye, Alexander Frapkin. I think I can say for certainly that I will never forget you."

"Adios, Mabra. I won't forget you either."

She enters the smoking darkness of the hall, and as she shuts the door I catch my last glimpse of her pretty face, half-covered by her raincoat collar. Her footsteps move away, vanishing into the sounds of a piano, a horn blowing outside on the street, children playing.

CHAPTER EIGHTEEN

WITH A SCREAM OF JOY Duke Blackstone dove straight for Shanahan's throat. Shanahan kicked hard, the soles of his size-twelve broughams connecting with Blackstone's face, flattening his nose and knocking out two teeth. Blackstone fell back and Shanahan went after him throwing a punch at his solar plexus, but Blackstone blocked it and kicked Shanahan in the balls. Shanahan dodged out of the way and

Rrrriiiinnnnngggggg.

Naturally somebody would call when I'm writing the most crucial scene in the book. I shouldn't answer, but it might be important.

"Hello?"

"Hello, Frapkin. This is Selma at Brunswick."

"Oh hi. I'm working on Shanahan right now. It's almost finished."

"I'm afraid I have bad news."

"Oh-oh."

"Ready?"

192

The Last Buffoon

"Go ahead."

"We declared bankruptcy today."

My eyes fill with kerosene, and my mind crumbles.

"Are you there?"

"I'm here."

"Can you speak a little louder?"

"I'm here!"

"I suggest you try to sell what you've written to Criterion. They've got a few cop series like Shanahan."

"I'll never go back to Criterion."

"Sure you will."

"Oh fuck."

"I want to wish you the best of luck with your career, despite our many disagreements over the years."

"Oh shit."

"I've got to call some more writers. Good luck, Frapkin."

I don't think I can get up from the chair. I'm finished. Brunswick was my last resort, and now it's gone. I can't go back to Criterion. I've come to the end of the line. Maybe the time has come for me to face the fact that I don't have what it takes to be a writer.

There's a fatal flaw in my character — I can see it now. I'm not an artist because I don't have the majesty of an artist. I'm just a petty stupid little man, a faker, a dud. I don't have it and I might as well admit it. It's time for me to move on to something else.

I think I'd like to get a job on a farm. It'd be nice to work in the dirt and grow tomatoes and corn and things. A simple honest life for a simple honest guy. And no more of this slaving over a typewriter and fighting the world single-handedly.

I've got it! I'll go to Israel and live on a kibbutz. I'll till the soil of my sacred homeland with no more worries and grandiose ambitions. This is the best idea I've had in years. I pick up the phone book, look up the number of the Israeli embassy, and dial.

"I'm interested in emigrating to Israel, and I wonder if you can give me some information."

"I'll switch you to the Aliyah desk," says a woman.

Pow.

"Aliyah."

"I'd like to emigrate to a kibbutz in Israel, and I was wondering if I could make the arrangements here in New York."

"How old are you?"

"Forty-two."

"I'm sorry, but the age limit for new members of kibbutzes is thirty-five."

"Oh shit!"

"What did you say?"

I hang up the phone. Now what do I do? Maybe I'd better go up on the roof where my psyche can spread out, and think things over.

I put on my field jacket and Irish hat, go out into the hallway, and climb the stairs to the roof. I push open the door, and straight ahead are rooftops, chimneys, and the sun shining on the steeple of Saint Anthony's Cathedral.

I pace around the roof, my hands in my jacket pockets. It's very beautiful up here, there's a nice breeze and the cool air is calming my mind. My problem is I can't write good books because I don't have the time, and I don't have the time because I don't write good books. Somehow I must break this vicious cycle. Maybe I should apply for a government grant.

I happen to glance into the apartment of the Japanese girl across the way, and she's lying on her bed in a corner, her feet pointed toward me. She's reading a book that's hiding her face, her dress is hiked up — and she's masturbating herself with her free hand! My throat tightens and balls start to foam. I've been lusting after her for these many years, and there she is playing with herself, right before my very eyes.

And — wait a minute! That bookjacket — I'd know that lurid artwork anywhere — twenty yards or twenty miles away. I clutch my thrashing heart in my hand because I realize that the book she's reading is none other than *Patti's Honeymoon* by Lancelot Wimbledon!

Oh my God! How am I to deal with this? There's only one thing to do. I must go over there, introduce myself, and offer to help. She'll probably call the cops, but what the hell, only in danger is there glory.

I run down to my apartment and look at myself in the bathroom mirror. I brush my hair, splash on a little English Leather, and gargle with Lavoris. Then I put on my Burberry and Borsalino, which show me to the best of my advantage.

I leave my apartment and bound down the stairs. At street level I run west on Christopher Street, south on Bedford, and east on Barrow. I reach the front of her building and pause to catch my breath, because I want to deliver my lines smoothly, directly from my diaphragm.

Although this maneuver is certain to fail like everything else I've done, I want it to be impeccable.

Ascending the stoop, I enter the hallway and press all the buttons, because in every New York apartment building there is always somebody waiting for somebody.

Sure enough the door buzzes back, and like a thief I enter the downstairs corridor. The stairs are to the left, covered with green carpeting. I begin to climb to the temple of the rising sun.

There's just one problem, and it's major. If she starts screaming for the police, and I flee, someone on a lower floor might stop me with a lead pipe. In that eventuality I'll go to jail and be disgraced, but of course Warmflash'll get me out on bail and then I'll kill myself. There's nothing to worry about.

But how wonderful it'd be to stick it to that Japanese girl. She's a real piece of ass — just my type. She's not American so she'd probably understand and even appreciate the sexuality of a real man.

I'm approaching the top floor. There are four doors, and hers must be the one farthest on the right. I walk on the green carpet to the sacred portal, pause, bite my lower lip, and read her name: Tamiko Ohashi. What lovely syllables. Well, I'd better get this over with. The Nos don't count — only the Yesses count. Grinding my teeth, I knock.

There's scurrying inside, then silence.

I knock louder.

Light footsteps come to the door. She must be looking through the peephole. "Who is it?" she asks in a high sharp voice.

196

The Last Buffoon

"Your neighbor from across the alley. I have to talk with you."

"What you want?"

"Open the door so I won't have to shout."

Locks are unsnapped and the door opens three inches, held to that distance by a thick gold chain. Behind it is Tamiko Ohashi, her eyes like a cat's, lips like a little pink flower, black bangs, and fear. "Yes?"

I smile as best I can. "I live in the apartment behind you, and I happened to be up on the roof just now, when I looked down and saw what you were doing. I thought you might want to know that — "

She slams the door in my face.

Okay, I expected that. I'll just go back to my office and apply for a federal grant.

I'm a few steps down when her door opens again. She's standing behind the chain, a little porcelain figure.

"Come here, please," she says.

I walk back and stop at the door.

She looks searchingly at my face. "You are the writer, are you not?"

"How do you know?" I stammer.

"I can see over there just like you can see over here."

I blink and swallow. "Oh."

"You work very hard."

"Maybe too hard."

"What is your name, please?"

"Alexander Frapkin."

"Say that again please, slowly. My English pronunciation is not so good."

197

"Al-ex-an-der Frap-kin."

"Mr. Frapkin, I am Miss Ohashi." She bows her head slightly.

"How do you do, Miss Ohashi."

"What do you write, Mr. Frapkin?"

"Novels."

"Do you get them published?"

"I've had about fifteen of them published."

"That many?"

"Yes."

"You must be very famous."

"No, I haven't been very successful so far."

"What do you write about?"

"All sorts of things."

"I have never met an American author before. Would you like to come in for a cup of tea?"

"I'd be delighted."

She smiles demurely, pulls the chain off the door, and opens it wide. I smell flowers and see on the wall a Japanese brushstroke painting of two wild horses. Koto music is being played, making the air quiver. I step forward and she closes the door with deft movements of her little hands. My head is spinning and my heart is thundering but somehow I must

HOLD ON!

The End

Afterword

THE LAST BUFFOON: what a strange book. The vulgarity is way over the top. It doesn't fit into any category. What kind of sick mind could write such a novel?

It was published in 1980 but actually written several years before. Believe it or not, it was conceived as my breakthrough novel, to establish me for all time as a great American novelist. Ah, the webs we weave.

I was deeply involved in writing pulp fiction at the time. It occurred to me that my crazy desperate life might be the basis for a novel in the tradition of other novels about mad artists such as THE GINGER MAN by J.P. Donleavy, THE HORSE'S MOUTH by Joyce Carey, and THE FAN MAN by my old friend William Kotzwinkle.

THE LAST BUFOON is not 100% autobiographical. I never masturbated in movie theaters. No one ever hung me out of a window by my heels. No one ever raped someone as a result of reading one of my novels, as far as I know. I never had a love affair with my Japanese neighbor, although she really existed and occasionally I saw her across the back alley between our Greenwich Village apartments.

Yet essentially THE LAST BUFFOON was a very true psychological portrait of my stressful life at the time, when I was living hand to mouth, and my publishers never paid me as stipulated in their own contracts. One of my editors, the great Peter McCurtin no less, told me once that if I wanted to get paid, I'd have to break into the office safe. When my bathroom window broke, my horrible landlord really did say, "Put your coat on."

Alexander Frapkin was me, exaggerated to the max. All my frustrations, confusions and warped insights were poured into the novel, twisted and spun to make them more freaky. Mabra was based on a real woman from Uruguay. We had a little romance, broke up, then she called one day, said she was having immigration problems, and asked if I'd marry her. I felt sorry for her so we went down to City Hall and got hitched. I didn't marry her for money but to help her remain in America, and also because I still loved her sort of. Unfortunately we had to live together and didn't get along well. Our values were very different to say the least. She thought I was a failure, loser and totally deluded fool. Based on the evidence, it was difficult to disagree. Some dialogue between Mabra and Frapkin was based on our actual interactions. But the true story became tragic because she died of breast cancer when she was around 28, while we still were still legally married but not living together.

My then literary agent, the magnificent Elaine Markson, was enthusiastic about THE LAST BUFFOON but unable to sell it. Several years later I convinced my new editor at Belmont-Tower, Milburn Smith, to publish it. He put a photo of me on the cover, standing in a trash barrel in Washington Square Park, where I probably belonged. It was published under my pseudonym Leonard Jordan.

After publication I received a lot of fan mail for THE LAST BUFFOON. Evidently many people really liked it. Two movie producers optioned the book but no movie ever was made. As I write these words on 7/15/2015, a Hollywood screenwriter has optioned the novel and presumably is writing a screenplay. I'm not getting my hopes up because the odds are against Frapkin leaping onto the silver screen. But the odds always are against Frapkin, yet he never gives up hope. He has faith in his talent despite all indications to the contrary.

Now THE LAST BUFFOON apparently has achieved the status of underground cult classic. I've found some used copies selling for $268.00. I'm very grateful to Devin Murphy for republishing it in paper for sale at reasonable cost. I hope it sells a zillion copies so that I can relocate to Paris and date dancers in the Folies Bergere.

— *Len Levinson*

About the Author

Phoro by Ray Block

LEN LEVINSON is the author of 83 novels written under 22 pseudonyms, published originally by Bantam, Dell, Fawcett, Harper, Jove, Charter Diamond, Zebra, Belmont-Tower, and Signet, among others. He has been acclaimed a "Trash Genius" by Paperback Fanatic magazine, and his books have sold an estimated two-and-one-half million copies.

Born 1935 in New Bedford, Massachusetts, he served on active duty in the U.S. Army 1954–1957, graduated from Michigan State University class of 1961, and relocated to New York City where he worked in advertising and public relations for ten years before becoming a full-time writer of novels.

He left NYC in 2003, residing first in Aurora, Illinois, and since 2004 in a small town (population 3,100) in rural northwest Illinois, surrounded by corn and soybean fields, way out on the Great American Prairie.

He has married twice, but presently lives alone with his MacBook Pro and a library of approximately three thousand books, which he studies assiduously in his never-ending effort to understand the meaning of life itself.

He has three novels and one non-fiction book in the pipeline.

17240577R00116

Printed in Great Britain
by Amazon